GHOST STORIES OF CANADA

Ghost Stories of Canada

Copyright © 1985 by Val Clery

All Rights Reserved

ISBN 0-88882-074-7

Publisher: Anthony Hawke
Designer: Gerard Williams
Composition: Accurate Typesetting Limited
Printer: Tri-Graphic Printing (Ottawa) Ltd.

Hounslow Press
A Division of
Anthony R. Hawke Limited
124 Parkview Avenue,
Willowdale, Ontario, Canada
M2N 3Y5

Printed in Canada

Second Printing 1988

Front Cover Photograph by Bill Brooks

Contents

"The outward and visible sign of an inward fear." That's how Ambrose Bierce defines a ghost in *The Devil's Dictionary*. We're most of us inclined to cling hopefully to some belief in a life hereafter, possibly a better life. On the other hand, because we're afraid of what we cannot know, we cling even more fiercely to the life we have here on earth. No matter how hard our lot has been, no matter how the body insists that it has had enough, we are always going to feel reluctant — as that phrase so aptly puts it — "to give up the ghost." We sense that our soul or spirit, with all its passions and memories, is certain to survive, so perhaps we're half-afraid of becoming one of those disembodied spirits tied to earth by unfinished business here.

Not surprisingly, most ghost stories concern spirits intent on righting some past wrong or on guarding some treasured place or object on earth. Those of us who have never encountered a ghost may be tempted to dismiss such stories as imaginary. And, in a sense, we may be right. What more effective way can there be for spirits to defy the laws of physics, to bridge the gulf between the material world and their world, than to manifest themselves in the imagination of those they wish to influence?

Until a few centuries ago the vastness of Canada was virtually empty. So it would be fair to wonder if Canada has many ghost stories to offer. But ghosts are no respecters of time or space: wherever men and women have lived there will be ghosts. Even the original Indians and Inuit of the North have always acknowledged the presence of spirits.

But are these stories true? In the shadowy half-world shared by imagination and memory, by fear and longing and doubt, where stories are exchanged by whispered word of mouth, there is no truth. Nothing is certain, nothing can be proved, nothing is real — these are ghost stories.

GHOST STORIES OF CANADA

VAL CLERY

1

The Doll

I got to know the Stetsons in England during the late sixties. Even though I'd never been to Canada, I was working as a radio producer for the London bureau of the CBC and most of my friends were Canadian freelance broadcasters and journalists. There were a lot of them in London because it was comparatively cheap to live there at the time and it was a good base for touring about in Europe.

The Stetsons were in their mid-twenties and recently married. Jack was completing work for a Ph.D in history and working part time for one of the news agencies on Fleet Street, and Sara, who'd worked for a newspaper in B.C., was freelancing for CBC whenever she could sell a story or an interview. They were an attractive couple: Jack, stocky and fair, tending to be a bit pompous and academic; Sara, slight, lively, and pretty, with long dark hair and a dry sense of humour.

They were making the best of their time abroad, working during the fall and winter so that they could take off during the summer for Spain or Yugoslavia or Morocco. I saw a lot of them because Sara used to come to me looking for commissions, and because they lived just around the corner from me in Notting Hill Gate. We'd usually get together in the local pub on Sundays and often met for dinner during the week. Although they were very relaxed and liberal, they were also quite conventional in outlook. Jack intended to go back and teach university in Canada, and Sara wanted to have a family and continue to work in broadcasting.

After three years Jack had completed his thesis, so they packed up and headed home. A couple of years later I heard that they were living in Ottawa and that Jack was lecturing at Carleton. Not long afterward I settled in Toronto as a radio producer. When I had to go up to Ottawa for a few days to cover a convention, I looked them up. They were renting a small house near the university. Jack, already an assistant professor, was taking himself rather too seriously. Sara, who was five months pregnant and looking prettier than ever, was getting

1

a lot of fun out of her condition. We spent a hilarious evening re-
miniscing about London and Europe.

Later I had a call from Jack to announce the birth of a son,
Timothy, and to complain that he hadn't been getting a lot of sleep.
After that, for a couple of years, our only contact was through
Christmas cards. But one day Jack called to say he was in town for a
conference and asked me to have lunch with him. For a change, he
didn't talk much about the university, apart from mentioning that he
was now an associate professor; but he did tell me a lot about the
wonders of his son, Timothy, who at two was well on his way to
being a prodigy. Moreover, in six months a second child would be
born. To accommodate this increase in the family, they'd just bought
an old house in the Gatineau Hills and would be moving out there the
following week. He invited me to visit them for a weekend in a couple
of months' time, during the summer.

Although I'm not too fond of country life, I was fond of the Stetsons, so I agreed to go. On a warm, calm July evening I flew up to
Ottawa, where Jack met me at the airport. He looked a little tired and
sounded more serious than usual as he greeted me with the usual
polite questions about the trip and how my work was going. As we
drove through the outskirts of the capital, across the Ottawa River,
and into Quebec, he said very little and answered my few questions
very briefly in an abstracted tone of voice, keeping his eyes fixed on
the road. I was puzzled.

It had been a showery spring and summer so far, so the rolling
countryside was still green and fresh-looking. We passed through a
couple of small villages, then turned down a side road and finally into
a long curving drive. The house, dappled with late-afternoon sun-
shine, was a charming old place — a two-storey stone-built main
section with a stucco wing added later, large sash windows with
green wooden shutters, and a stout green door. Set on a large lot that
sloped down to a small stream, it was surrounded by a stand of tall
maples, and there was an immense weeping willow on the front
lawn.

"Impressive," I remarked. Jack shrugged and smiled stiffly.

Hearing the car, Sara opened the front door and stepped out. She
smiled broadly as I got out of the car and came forward to give me a
hug and a kiss.

"Welcome to the Stetson estate," she said. She'd obviously dressed for the occasion and was wearing a pale blue linen dress full
enough to hide her figure. She had cut her hair short, and, although
the prettiness was still there, her face had a strained look about it, and
there were slight mauve crescents below her eyes.

"You'll have to wait until the morning to meet Tim," she added as
she led the way indoors. "He gets sort of worn down in the hot
weather."

"So we can have dinner in peace," said Jack.

While Sara went to finish cooking. Jack led me upstairs to my room in the wing, giving me a brief tour of the rambling house as we went. Naturally, as a historian, he'd found out a great deal about the house and its past. The stone section had been built in 1856 for a Quebec doctor named Archand and his family. It had obviously become a large family, for the doctor was obliged to add the wing two generations later, in 1893. In 1917 the two eldest sons of a third generation were killed in France, and the house was sold two years later to a Quebec politician, whose family occupied it until 1961, when it was sold to a civil servant with External Affairs. When he was assigned to Moscow, he put the house on the market and the Stetsons bought it.

Jack admitted ruefully that he could never have afforded the place on his present salary. Fortunately, his father, who was a dentist, had agreed to lend them the money they needed. Sara's sense of style was evident throughout the house, and they'd obviously spent a great deal of time and money in making the place just right. Maybe that explained the strain and weariness I sensed in them both.

Sara, who always excelled at everything she attempted, had prepared quite a marvelous meal. Conversation, awkward at first, as though we were new acquaintances, was soon warmed by the wine and my appreciation of every dish she set on the table. By the time we were sitting over coffee and Armagnac, something like our original intimacy had returned. They both admitted that in buying the house they might have bitten off more than they could chew. It was crazy, because until Tim and the new kid were at school there was no hope of Sara getting back into broadcasting and earning some extra income.

"Unless," Sara remarked, "we get ourselves an *au pair*."

Jack frowned at this suggestion but said nothing. Sensing a point of tension between them, I said with a laugh, "Well, to get the most out of this mansion, you'll have to have as many offspring as the original owner."

"No way," said Jack with a heavy sigh. "Two will be more than enough." Sara gave him a worried glance.

We dropped the subject and talked of other things until after midnight. We reminisced about the past we had enjoyed together, exchanged gossip about mutual friends of those days, and Jack and I compared the bureaucratic horrors of academe and broadcasting. When these topics and the Armagnac were exhausted, we all agreed it was time for bed.

As I slipped into my very comfortable bed, it occurred to me that something about the house made me uneasy. I knew it had nothing to do with my ingrained dislike of the rural lifestyle. The house, because of the Stetsons' appreciation of the good life at any cost, confronted me with none of the expected discomforts; it was as charming inside as it had seemed from the outside. Was it something about the family rather than the house that was disturbing? Those hints of tension between friends whom I had always thought to be a perfect match? It was just as I was falling asleep that it struck me that in all our talk

there had been very little mention of Timothy, no echoes of the paren-
tal pride and joy that Jack had expressed to me only two months
before. Strange, I thought, strange. . . .

I was awakened, I don't know how much later, by the far-off
sound of a child throwing a temper tantrum. I heard the rustle of
footsteps and the hushed, calming voice of Sara. It took sometime for
the sobs to die away, and then I drifted back to sleep.

A sound awakened me again. The angle of sunlight in the room
suggested it was still quite early — too early. The door was ajar, and a
child stood in the gap. It wasn't hard to identify the intruder as
Timothy: he'd inherited his mother's slight physique and her dark
hair and complexion, and his father's grey-green eyes. He was hugging a large grubby rag doll, its long arms and legs dangling limply.

"Hello," I said. "You're Tim, aren't you?"

"Yes," he said slowly. "Who are you?"

"Oh, I'm a friend. Is it time to get up?"

"Yes. You're a lazybones. We're going to play now. 'Bye."

He turned away, closing the door after him. I took my time getting
out of bed and showering, just in case the wake-up visit had merely
been Tim's idea. I could hear movements downstairs as I began to
shave, so I assumed Sara and Jack were already up.

As I was drying my face, I heard the kid throwing another tantrum
and Sara trying to calm him. The wails diminished, but when I
glanced out the bedroom window I saw Tim lying on the lawn, kicking the turf in temper.

I got dressed slowly and headed downstairs. As I reached the top
of the staircase, I heard Jack and Sara arguing loudly. Sara was saying, "But I tell you, while you were at the airport yesterday I sneaked
it away from him. And I locked it in that trunk in the attic. He
couldn't have got it out."

"Well, how the hell did he get it then?" Jack said.

"How do I know? It's like the other times."

"For God's sake, I don't believe this stuff. . . ."

There was a pause, so I began to descend the stairs as noisily as I
could. When I reached the front hallway, Sara called out, "We're in
here."

The kitchen was large and sunny. Sara, working at the stove,
threw me a quick bright smile. Jack, standing at the window, said
with forced heartiness, "So the country air got to you, eh?"

"No," I said, "the Armagnac got to me. That's really strong stuff."

"The coffee's made," Sara said, "and the rest'll be along in a moment. We're going to eat outside."

Outside proved to be a delightful terrace along the back of the
house, shaded by a vine-covered trellis.

While Sara carried breakfast out from the kitchen, Jack went off in
search of Tim. I was sipping my first cup of coffee when they emerged
from beneath the trees, hand in hand.

"Hi, Tim," I called out. "Y'see, I'm not a lazybones."

Sara looked puzzled.

"He came to wake me up," I explained.

"Not too early?"

"Of course not. It's such a gorgeous day."

Tim, still looking a shade tearful, set to work on a bowl of cereal.

"We thought we might drive into Ottawa this morning," Sara said. "We can stroll around the market and have brunch somewhere. And Tim and I have to do some shopping, haven't we, Tim?"

Tim, still spooning his cereal, nodded uncertainly. When he had finished, he slipped down from his chair and, without a word, wandered off among the trees.

"Still shy of strangers," Jack remarked apologetically. "The move out here was tough on him. All his friends are in Ottawa."

"I can't wait till he's old enough for kindergarten," Sara added.

"Well, he'll have a new playmate soon," Jack said, reaching over to pat Sara's stomach. She made a face.

The warm sunlight, the peace of the countryside, scrambled eggs and crisp bacon, and plenty of good coffee restored our mood of the previous evening and soon we were happily gossiping and joking again, reluctant to stir from the breakfast table. Eventually, however, Tim reappeared to ask when we were going to go, so we had to get ready.

The drive into Ottawa was uneventful, and we spent more than an hour roaming around the lively farmers' market, a cornucopia of the summer produce of Quebec and the Ottawa Valley. We ran into a number of the Stetsons' Ottawa friends and even a couple whom we all had known in London. In the end we settled in for a late brunch in a sea-food restaurant in the market. Again, Bloody Marys, clam chowder, steamed mussels, and salad stimulated our sense of friendship. However, after a time, Tim became restless and threw another tantrum. I couldn't quite make out, between his wails, what he was fussing about, but in the end Sara announced that she and Tim would go off and do some shopping and meet us in the parking lot an hour later.

Jack sighed as he watched his son leave. "He's at a difficult age," he said.

We finished brunch slowly and then passed the time browsing in a local bookstore. Sara and Tim were already waiting by the car when we arrived at the parking lot. Tim was carrying a large new teddy bear but not looking very much happier. I managed to coax a smile from him on the drive home by inventing improbable names for the new toy.

The rest of the afternoon was spent lolling in the garden, reading newspapers and magazines, and chatting. Sara and Jack took turns entertaining Tim, pushing him in a swing under the trees, playing catch with him, and fishing in the stream with a makeshift rod and line, without catching anything. The new teddy bear lay ignored on the terrace.

Jack had made a dinner reservation for us at a nearby auberge, and, in the early evening as we were having drinks, the daughter of a neighbour arrived on a bicycle to babysit. She managed to occupy Tim's attention as we drove off.

The restaurant was crowded and noisy, but the food and wine were excellent. We enjoyed ourselves until late in the evening, when Sara went to phone home to check if all was well. She returned to the table looking worried.

"Trouble?" Jack asked quickly.

"Not now," she said. "He acted up quite a bit when it was bed-time. But she's just managed to get him to sleep."

There was an awkward pause, then Sara said to me, "You must think Tim is an awful brat. It's only recently. . . ."

"As they say, it's only a stage," I said. "Maybe, if he knows another kid is coming, that's upsetting him. They say the firstborn don't like the competition."

"Well, maybe," she said doubtfully, "But he seemed really pleased when I told him first. Back in Ottawa. . . ."

Jack rather obviously changed the subject and we continued with our meal. Although they went out of their way to try to seem relaxed, I sensed that they were both on edge and anxious to get home.

On the drive home, using the pretext of having some work to do, I told them I'd like to catch a noon plane back to Toronto. I found the situation too uncomfortable to take for another full day.

As it turned out, there were no further upsets during the night, and in the morning, during breakfast and afterward, Tim seemed an ordinary, amusing three-year-old. I half-regretted having said I'd leave early.

Jack said he had to pick up some papers for marking at his office, so, after dropping him off at the campus, Sara drove me to the air-port, with Tim sitting quietly in the backseat.

Before boarding my plane, I thanked her profusely and convinc-ingly, I thought, for a wonderful weekend.

"Maybe I can come back when the next offspring arrives," I said. "I wouldn't mind being a godfather."

She laughed and said that so I could be. She'd let me know the moment it happened. I gave them each a hug and headed off, waving to Tim as I went. He didn't wave back.

Four months later, not having heard from the Stetsons, I called Jack's office at the university and left a message. He didn't return my call. I tried again a couple of weeks later. There was no call back. That worried me. Had I offended them somehow? Or were they still hav-ing problems? Before Christmas I sent them a card, with the message, "Am I a godfather yet?" and an illustrated book about teddy bears for Tim. There was no response, so I thought I'd better leave the matter to them.

It was the following summer, almost a year since I'd visited them in Quebec, that I saw Sara. I was hurrying through the lobby of the

CBC radio building, late for a program recording, when I glimpsed her out of the corner of my eye. She was standing by the window where the performers picked up their paychecks. I sensed that she'd noticed me and had turned away. She looked much paler and thinner than when I'd last seen her. I walked over.

"Sara! What are you doing here?"

She looked at me, pretending to be surprised.

"Oh, working. I . . . I'm back on the air."

"Great. Have you all moved here?"

"No," she said quietly, avoiding my eyes.

"Look, I'm late for a recording. Can we have lunch? Today?"

She hesitated, then said, "Yes, I suppose we should."

"Won't be finished until two. What about across the road at the Four Seasons? In the restaurant?"

"That's fine. I'll be there."

I squeezed her shoulder and she managed to smile.

There weren't many people left in the restaurant when I arrived. She was sitting at the far end, at a table by the window, nursing a drink and looking small and lonely.

I bent over to kiss her cheek, saying, "I'm still bewildered, Sara."

"Why wouldn't you be?" she said with a slight shrug.

"But what's going on?"

"We broke up. Jack is living in Ottawa again. I moved here. It's easier to get work."

"And the children?"

"Child," she said. "Tim is with me here."

"But I don't understand."

She looked very dejected and said slowly, "It's a long sad story. But I suppose you should hear it. After all, you. . . ."

She broke off because a waiter had arrived to take my order, and waited until he had gone.

"You were there almost at the beginning of it, although you may not have realized it, last summer when you came to visit."

"Well, I did sense then that there was something not right between you and Jack. But I couldn't make out what was wrong."

"How could you have? It was something you'd never have imagined. You'll have to bear with me. . . ."

She was silent for several minutes, staring down at her drink.

"I'd have to say I brought it all on myself," she went on. "Even though I felt there was something bad about that house the moment I walked into it, there was so much I liked about it that I ignored the feeling. The people who'd lived in it before us, the External Affairs couple, had left it in very good shape, but we worked on it for a month before we moved in, and another couple of months afterward. I wanted it to be perfect."

"And it seemed to be," I said.

"The day we moved in, I drove down early by myself, to make sure that everything was just right. And it was — spick-and-span. I'd made out lists of where everything was to go, and I walked around every room to make sure I hadn't missed anything. When I walked into the room we'd chosen for Tim, there was this thing in the middle of the floor. It was a big rag doll, a horrible ugly thing. And it frightened me. It was made of some sort of coarse material, like canvas, stained and greasy, crudely stitched together, with a mouth and eyes and nose and hair embroidered on the head with black wool, I couldn't imagine where it had come from. And I could scarcely bring myself to touch it. But then I felt so angry that it was there at all that I grabbed it and threw it onto the top shelf of a closet. It was much heavier than it looked, probably stuffed with sawdust instead of rags. A few moments later, I heard the moving van coming up the drive. Jack had come down with it, to show the way. The day was so frantic that I forgot all about the doll. We worked until we were exhausted and then just fell into bed.

"We'd left Tim with friends of ours in Ottawa who had kids. The next day, when we'd got everything in some sort of order, I drove over in the afternoon and picked him up. He was very excited about the move and explored every inch of the house and the garden. We had quite a job persuading him to settle down and sleep. And we were still so wiped out that we wanted to get to bed ourselves.

"I woke up quite early to hear Tim moving about in his room and talking. Because I was three months pregnant I wasn't at my best in the mornings, so I just lay there for an hour or so, listening to Tim and wondering what he was up to. Eventually I got myself up and went to Tim's room. He was sitting on the floor, with that big ugly doll on his knees, talking to it. You know how you read about people being seized by a feeling of dread? Well, at that moment, a chill ran through me and I began to shudder as I looked at that doll. Tim was so absorbed that he didn't even notice me coming in. Somehow I managed to grab it from him. I ran out of the room with it, threw it into a storage closet in the corridor, and locked it in. Tim threw a tantrum. You heard what he was like when you came down. But I managed to calm him down — I can't think what I promised him — before he woke Jack.

"But for the rest of the morning, Tim was a real pain, cranky and demanding. It was quite unlike him. He'd always been an easy kid with a great sense of fun, able to entertain himself for hours on end. Jack was puzzled and short-tempered with him, which didn't make things easier. I knew I'd have to tell Jack about the doll, and so, when I'd settled Tim down for a nap after lunch, I told Jack exactly what had happened.

"Well, you know Jack, the ultimate pragmatist. For him there's always a rational explanation for everything. He thought the doll was just the one thing we'd overlooked when we were clearing the place out. And as for Tim getting hold of the doll out of the closet — well, Tim was bright, inquisitive, he'd probably pulled a chair over to the closet and dragged it down somehow. I knew he couldn't possibly have reached it, but I didn't say so. I told him to go up and look at the doll himself, in the storage closet. When he came down, he agreed that it was really a horrible-looking thing, but he thought it might be a valuable antique. He felt we should let Tim play with it, as long as it kept him happy. He was bound to get bored with it, and then we could get rid of it. I agreed, but I wish I never had."

"I saw that doll," I said, "and it certainly wasn't pretty. Tim was carrying it when he woke me the first morning of my visit."

"Oh yes," she said, "that was another crisis. For the couple of months before you arrived, we'd allowed Tim to play with that awful doll. I'll have to admit that it seemed to work. For Tim. He'd spend hours in his room, playing and talking to the doll. And of course he took it with him everywhere. As far as I was concerned, I couldn't get rid of my feeling of revulsion for it. I couldn't bring myself to handle it, and I found it hard even to look at it. I loved that house, and our life there could have been nearly perfect, but the presence of that doll was a blot of evil that seemed to spoil everything. The day before you arrived, I told Jack I couldn't take it anymore; we'd have to get rid of the doll. He was doubtful about that, but he agreed, because he knew how it was affecting me. So, when Jack was picking you up at the airport, I managed to get Tim to sleep early and to sneak the doll out of his bed. I should have destroyed it, and I don't know why I didn't, but I locked it in a trunk in the attic."

"And the next morning he managed to get hold of the doll again," I said.

"Yes. You saw it. It was very frightening. Before you came down for breakfast, I took it from him and hid it again. In the freezer, as a matter of fact. And of course Tim was impossible that weekend. You saw it yourself. And buying him that teddy bear didn't work. He never played with it. And it was more than Jack could handle. So, when we got back from taking you to the airport and when we'd managed to get Tim to bed, I insisted that Jack take the doll out to the incinerator — we didn't have garbage collection — and burn it. I went with him. He soaked it in barbecue starter and I stood there and watched until it was just a pile of ashes. I can't tell you the relief I felt."

I asked her if she'd like to order lunch. She shook her head. "But I could use another drink," she said. I signalled the waiter.

"But that wasn't the end of the story." she said. "The next three months were absolute hell. Tim was a demon, acting up all the time. And Jack blamed me for being too hasty. And my pregnancy wasn't going well. In the end, my obstetrician insisted that I go into the hospital for the last three weeks.

"A few days after I went in, Jack brought Tim in to visit me. I was astonished. Tim seemed himself again, very affectionate. But Jack looked exhausted. I thought he must be finding it a strain coping on his own, although a sitter came to look after Tim during the day.

"The baby was two weeks late. And the delivery was very difficult. She was a small baby ... perfect ... beautiful ... very lively. Suzanne ..."

She stopped speaking and closed her eyes. Tears trickled down her pale face.

"You don't have to go on," I said quietly.

She shook her head. "I have to tell someone sometime." she said, dabbing her eyes dry.

"Tim was fascinated by the baby, and very gentle with her. And he seemed delighted the day we came home. But Jack seemed very strange and tense. I should have guessed. As soon as he had a chance, he told me. It had turned up again — the doll. I couldn't believe what he was saying. I was speechless. And terrified. He said the night after I'd gone into the hospital, he woke up and heard Tim moving about in his room. He got up and went in there. Tim was sitting on the floor in the moonlight, just as I'd first seen him, with the doll on his knees, talking to it. Jack couldn't bring himself to do anything. He just went back to bed and lay there until morning, feeling utterly beaten. And that's how I felt then. We just stared at each other, feeling there was nothing more we could do.

"For three weeks it seemed almost as though we could learn to accept the situation. Mostly Tim kept the doll in his own room, and a lot of the time he just watched me feeding and bathing and changing Suzanne. But there wasn't a moment when I wasn't conscious of that doll in the house. And it was the same for Jack."

She stopped again, looking very white, her fingers clenched around her glass.

"This is the hard part," she said softly, and took a sip of her drink.

"One morning I woke up. It was already light. Suzanne always woke up for a very early feeding. There was no sound. I knew immediately that something dreadful had happened. I was so terrified my legs seemed numb. The nursery door was open. Tim was sitting on the floor in a corner. The doll was in the crib, lying on top of her. I flung it away. Suzanne's face was very dark, convulsed. And cold. I screamed and screamed. Jack came. We tried to get her to breathe again. It was no use. It was too late...."

I reached over and held her hand. She nodded, her eyes closed and her lips moving.

"Jack called the doctor," she went on. "I just sat there, hugging that cold, still little body, and Jack stood and stared out the window. I hadn't noticed, but Tim and the doll were gone. We could hear him talking to it in his room.

"We didn't tell the doctor anything about that. He was very kind. Crib death, he said. And he gave me a sedative. I put Suzanne back in her crib and covered her up. Then I went back to bed. When I woke up, Jack told me he'd taken the doll from Tim and chopped it into pieces with an axe. Then he'd cut a hole in the ice and thrown the pieces in the stream. I think I must have laughed at him when he told me that. It didn't matter."

She shrugged and glanced around the restaurant. We were the only people left.

"That was the end of it for us. It was so obvious to us both that we hardly bothered to discuss it. Jack blamed himself entirely. Why I can't imagine. But it was clear that Tim reminded him of what had happened so unbearably that he just couldn't take it. We sold the house and went our separate ways. And so here I am."

"And Tim," I asked, "how has he been?"

"Bright," she said, "a good kid. Star of the kindergarten, and never any trouble. The three of us get along just fine now."

"I don't follow you...."

"Oh, the day we moved into our apartment here, it was there again, lying on the floor. Always will be, I suppose. Unless Tim grows out of dolls."

2

Death on the Ice

It was quite a few years ago, when the protests against the Newfoundland seal hunt were just beginning. I'd come from Toronto to produce a radio documentary about the hunt and got stranded in St. Anthony, on the northeast tip of the island.

I'd already been out to the Front, as it was called, the vast field of drifting ice out in the Atlantic on which the harp seals give birth to their pups, the whitecoats that are the prey of the sealing fleet.

It hadn't been a pretty sight out there, and couldn't have been for anyone not used to it. The helplessness of the bawling newborn seal pups, the lumbering panic of their mothers, and the remorseless efficiency of the sealers composed a waking nightmare on the ice: the dazzling white landscape stained with vivid red blood and scattered with abandoned skinned carcases. the bundles of dripping pelts swinging through the air as they were winched aboard the ships, and the slush of blood and seal fat on the decks.

It was hard to remain as detached about the hunt as we were expected to be, but the two reporters I'd been working with, both Newfoundlanders, had been doing a good job, collecting the sounds of the hunt on their tape-recorders and cajoling interviews from sealers, most of whom were surly and suspicious because they were convinced that we'd present in a bad light what was for them a hard but necessary means of supplementing a poor livelihood.

We'd already taped most of the material we needed for the program, and I'd flown back to St. Anthony on a Fisheries Department helicopter, leaving the two reporters at work on the Front. I'd meant to go back out, but by the time I'd arranged to have the first batch of tapes shipped down to St. John's, the helicopter had taken off again. So I was stuck in St. Anthony until my reporters returned.

The hotel was overcrowded with bored newspapermen who'd been sent out in hope of a story about the anti-sealing protest, which never really developed. I didn't want to get into any arguments on that question, so I decided to take a stroll through the town. There wasn't much to the place, and when I reached the end of the main street, I followed a road up toward a headland overlooking the bay and the Atlantic, which were the colour of steel under a low, threatening sky. But it wasn't cold and there was very little wind.

I paused opposite the last house on the road and stared out across the sea. The glistening edge of the ice field was just visible far out in the gloom. What a way to have to earn a few extra dollars, I thought.

"'Tis mild then for March," a voice called out from behind me. "There'll be a storm."

I looked around. An erect, elderly man was standing in the open doorway of the house. He had stiff grey hair, but strong eyebrows, still dark, gave his weathered face a touch of youthfulness. He was wearing heavy trousers and a flannel workshirt.

"I'm glad I'm not out on that ice then," I said, walking toward him.

"Oh, they'll not be staying out there long. By now most of them has their quotas, so I hear."

We both stood gazing out into the hazy distance.

"You're up from St. John's?" he asked.

"No. From Toronto."

He nodded. "A fair ways to come. Are you writing for the papers?"

"No. I work for a radio program. I was out on the Front this morning, recording. Missed the helicopter back out there."

He nodded again, stroking his jaw.

"Would you care to come in and have a cup of tea?"

I thanked him and said I would. He beckoned me indoors, took my coat, and hung it up. It was a small, cozy place, the kitchen so neat that I guessed he must live by himself. He pulled out a chair for me beside the table. A kettle of tea was already brewing on the stove, and when he'd poured us each a cup, strong and black, he sat down himself.

"So, and what did you make of the swiling?"

"Swiling?" I asked.

"That's the old-time word for sealing in these parts," he explained. "Seals is known as swiles."

"It's a tough way to earn a living."

"Aye, it is that. A bad business for man and beast."

"I suppose you used to go out there yourself?"

He was filling a pipe from a pouch of tobacco.

"Only once," he said, "when I was a lad. And that was a long time ago. I never went on the ice after that."

"Now that I've seen what it's like out there, I'd hardly blame you."

He glanced at me for a moment, then lit his pipe.

"Oh, you get used to all that, the blood and the cold and the risk of it. Besides, in those days you weren't thought much of a man hereabouts if you didn't go swiling."

As he spoke I noticed through the window the first feathery flakes of snow drifting out of the grey sky.

"Far as I was concerned, there wasn't much choice," he went on, puffing at his pipe. "Me dad lost his life out on the Front when I was only five years old. That was way back in 1914, a terrible year. One ship, the *Southern Cross*, went down with all hands in a storm, a hundred and eighty men. And eighty more, me dad amongst them was lost on the ice in the same storm. A certain captain at the time, Abram Kean, was held to blame for leaving those men on the ice, but he had too much political pull for anyone to touch him."

He poured more tea and went on.

"They were hard times for the family after that, me mother and me younger sister and meself. By the time I was thirteen I was fishing. And before I was sixteen I went swiling, for the first and last time. Me mother tried to stop me, of course, but she knew it was no use. You had to have a ticket to get a berth on a sealing ship. I lied about me age to get one, and, as luck would have it, I shipped out with that same captain, Abram Kean. He must've known who I was, 'cause he always seemed to know every fishing family on the island. Likely he thought my shipping out with him took some of the blame off him for me dad's death."

He paused again to stare out at the snow falling thick and soft.

"That year the weather was much as it is now. A lot of late snow, and the ice was tight-packed and a long ways south. If you were with Cap'n Kean, you were counted to have a good berth, 'cause there wasn't a better man for finding the main patch, which is where the most seals would be found. Year after year Abram Kean would bring in the most pelts, and in his lifetime they say he brought in more than a million.

"It was slim pickings when we got to the Front. The ice was heavy and rafting up agin the bows whenever we made a move. We came on a few small patches of seals, but never brought in more than a hundred or so pelts a day for the first few days. It made it easy for me, at least, to find out what swiling was all about. Easy, I say, but it was hard for me at first to belt them little whitecoats with a club and sculp the pelts off of them while they were still hot. The watch master knew me father and he looked after me and showed me the ropes. It didn't take long to get used to the smell of the blood and fat; you lived with it sleeping and waking. And all for the chance of making a couple of hundred dollars, if you was lucky.

"After we'd been out four days, it began to look as if we'd be lucky if we got ten dollars, much less a hundred. No matter which way we turned, the ice was packed tight, and we was still taking only a couple of hundred pelts a day. According to the old hands, in a good year you might take twenty times that. Up on the bridge, you could see the Old Man — that's what we called Cap'n Kean, was fit to be tied.

"On the fourth night, the wind shifted around and by first light the ice began to open up a bit, so we was soon under way. But you could see by the sky that there was a storm coming up, and likely snow. There was a lot of open water to the southwest and that was the way we headed along the Front. Now and again we'd spot a small patch of swiles, but we just passed them by. Word came down that the Old Man was certain he knew where the main patch would be, and nobody doubted him, for he had a great gift for knowing that. Sure enough, early that afternoon, the barrelman, on lookout up on the mainmast, yelled down, 'We're in the fat, boys, swiles by the thousand, dead ahead.'

"We hove to, and with the engine stopped you could hear the whitecoats howling out on the ice. 'Go to it, me sons,' was all the Old Man had to say, and in a few minutes we were over the side, loaded down with gaffs and flagpoles and ropes.

"It was hard going. The wind'd cut through you, and the ice pans was buckling and shifting, so you had to watch your step, jumping from one to the next. As we was heading towards where we could hear the swiles, the watch master yelled out to me, 'Mind you stay close by me, boy, there'll be snow before night. And your mother'd never forgive me if I lost you.'

"It was near an hour before we got to the patch of swiles, 'cause the ice was buckled up in big ridges you had to climb over. With the threat of a storm we didn't waste any time getting to work on the patch of swiles. 'Twas hard, brutal work, though I'd been blooded already. The old hands could kill and sculp three whitecoats for every one I did, but everyone was too hard at it to notice anyone else.

"We'd sculped well nigh five hundred pelts when the snow began, and there was no shortage of whitecoats close by. The watch master told me to start tying the pelts into bundles — yaffles was the name they went by — and dragging them over to the nearest open water, which was about half-a-mile away over rough ice. And he told me to set up a flagpole where I left them so the ship could see it and come to pick up the pelts and ourselves before night set in. It was real hard work, dragging them pelts over the rough ice in that wind, with the snow cutting your face. And the snow was getting worse. I'd dragged four yaffles over to a big ice pan near the water, and the next time I turned back to where the men were killing, I couldn't see them or hear a sound because the snow was coming down that thick.

"There was a fresh trail of blood on the ice where I'd dragged the pelts, and I began to follow that, not able to see more than a few feet in front of me with the driving snow. Then I couldn't see the trail anymore. The snow had covered it over. I scraped around in the snow with me gaff, trying to find the trail. But it was no use. I was lost. I called out till I hadn't a breath left in me, but the wind swept me voice away: I was terrible afraid, terrible afraid. All alone there in the snow with night coming on . . . ."

He raised his eyes to stare out at the dusk beyond and the swirling snow catching the light from the window.

"Most other men going swiling," he went on, "would buy themselves a cheap compass to help them get their bearings on the ice. But we was too hard up for that, and I never had the heart to ask me mother for the extra money. I did the best I could to calm meself down. Then I went ahead slowly and carefully looking for a trace of the trail and trying in my mind to walk a straight line, with the wind in my face. It was no use and it was getting terrible dark. I was walking for what seemed like hours, falling over many's the time on the rough ice. Not a sign of man or beast. And I could feel the strength going out of me. I came to a big high-pressure ridge, you must've seen them out there on the Front, reared up ten feet or more. And I knew I hadn't the strength to get over it. But at least it protected me from the wind, which was cutting through me. So I cut a little cave into the ice there with me gaff, stuck the gaff pole in the ice, and lay down in that little hole. I had a bit of hard tack in me lunch bag and I chawed on that for a while. I began to feel a bit warmer at least. . . .Have you ever been in the fix that you thought you was going to die?"

"No, not really," I said. "I've been lucky."

He nodded, rubbing his face thoughtfully.

"It's not as bad as you'd imagine. When I was lying there that night, I could feel sleep creeping up over me, I'd heard tell that you should never let yourself go to sleep out in the cold like that, else you'd never wake up again. I knew I couldn't stop meself sleeping and I knew I'd likely die out there. I wasn't even sixteen yet, but, you know, I wasn't afraid and I didn't care. The last thing I remember thinking as I was drifting off was, leastways I'll see me dad again.

"I don't know to this day how long I slept there. When I woke up I was afraid to open me eyes, thinking maybe I'd passed on and was someplace else. And when I did open me eyes, I was certain I had passed on. The snow had stopped and there wasn't a breath of wind. The moon was big in the sky, very close, and everything looked shining silver. But I was still crouched in that hole I'd dug meself and I was aching hungry. I began shaking so bad that me teeth were chattering together.

"Then I noticed something strange. There was five whitecoats lying on the ice only a few feet from me, not one of them moving. For a while I thought I was imagining them there. I closed me eyes again and when I opened them the whitecoats was still there. I remembered I'd heard once that when men'd be out on the ice and real hungry, they'd cut open a pup and eat its heart raw. And I remembered too that someone had told me that the pelts were so fat that you could set light to them and keep yourself warm.

"I lay thinking about that, still shivering, not sure whether I was dead or dreaming. In the end I decided I was going to kill one of them whitecoats. I was so stiff, I could hardly move arm or leg. But in the end I managed to get onto me knees, and I was watching them whitecoats all the time, sure they'd take fright and make off where I couldn't catch them. I'd lost me club, but me gaff was stuck in the ice a few feet away and I slowly edged over towards it. I was just reaching out for it when one of the swiles raised its head and looked over at me.

"I near fell down on the ice. The face I saw on that pup, small though it was, was a man's face, a face I knew well. It was my father's face. Not that I remembered him when he was alive, but because me mother had a photo of him on a cabinet in the kitchen at home and often since he died I would stand and look at it.

"Then I heard a soft voice speaking. And it was a voice I remembered well from when I was small, me dad's voice. He always spoke soft. It was saying, 'So you came out on the ice, me son, like your dad. You should've had more sense.'

"Fear took a hold of me. I tried to get onto my feet and grab hold of the gaff, but me legs went from under me and I fell over on the ice.

"'No, son, no,' the voice said, 'you can't kill them as is dead already. Don't be afraid. We'll save you and look after you out here. In the long run, Abram Kean'll come back to find you. Black as his heart is, he'd not dare leave both father and son to die out here on the ice.'

"All the strength had gone out of me and I couldn't stir. I was certain in me mind I was dying or already dead. Then I heard a slithering sound, and next thing I knew them whitecoats had come all around me right up close and I could feel the heat of them through my clothes.

"My father's voice began speaking again. It was saying, 'There, son, that'll keep the life in you. I remember when I was about your age an old woman telling me that the souls of men that died out on the ice went into whitecoats until their time came to go to their rest. And I laughed in her face. Well, 'tis true, we know that now, me and those four men that died along with me out here. We'll not rest till the man as left us out here to die, dies himself and faces up to us.'

"I don't know whether I fainted then or just went to sleep. But I can remember feeling warm and happier than I'd felt before or since. And I don't know yet how many days or hours passed with me lying out on the ice with them whitecoats up against me.

"When I woke up, it was daylight, with the sun shining down on me, but it was still powerful cold. A ship's whistle, which must've wakened me in the first place, sounded again. I raised me head and, sure enough, not more than a couple of hundred yards away, butting through the ice, was Cap'n Kean's ship. I got up on me feet and waved me arms. The whistle sounded twice again and some men standing at the bow yelled to me.

"I looked down at the whitecoats lying around where I was standing. They looked like ordinary swiles now. I thought to meself, it was all just a dream you were having. But one of the whitecoats raised its head up and I heard me dad's quiet voice again, saying. 'You mind to tell Abram Kean, me son, we's waiting for him out here whenever his time comes.' 'I will, dad,' I said and grabbed me gaff and set off over the ice towards the ship.

"The ship was hove to now and two men came down the side sticks onto the ice and started running towards me. As they came near, I saw that one of them was the watch master. He yelled out to me, 'You're alive then, boy! We was certain you was lost!'

"When they reached me, they grabbed me arms to help me along, but I told them I'd be all right. 'You're alive, boy,' the watch master kept repeating, 'You're alive. You've been out on the ice three days, and look at you — good as new. It's a miracle, boy!'

"I got over to the ship and up the side sticks without help from either of them, the whole watch standing along the rails and calling out to me. When I came over the side, I saw the Old Man standing above on the bridge. He yelled out to the watch master, 'You bring that boy up here, mister.'

"So I went aloft on the bridge with the watch master. I could see straight away that the cap'n was in a rage. He stood glaring at me for a minute or two, then he said, 'So you go and get yourself lost, boy, first time out on the ice. And you lose us nigh on half a day's swiling looking for you. How you're alive still is a mystery to me. The good Lord must've taken pity on you, which is more'n I'd be willing to do.'

"He walked over to the wing of the bridge and looked to where I'd been lying, then he said to me, 'I'll tell you what you're going to do now, boy. You're going to get back on that ice and you're going to sculp them five whitecoats you left lying out there, so's we can see if there's the making of a man in you at all. Now go to it!'

"I just stood and stared back at him, then I said, 'I'll not touch them swiles, for it's them that kept me alive.'

"He looked at me as if he couldn't believe his ears. 'You'll do as I say, boy, or you'll never get a berth on this ship or any other ship as long as you live.'

"I just stood me ground and shook me head. 'Cap'n Kean,' I said, 'I've a message for you. When I was out on that ice, I saw me father. And he told me to tell you that he and four other men you left to die out there'd be waiting for you when your time comes.'

"For a minute I thought the Old Man was going to belt me. He raised up his fist, shaking with rage. Then just as sudden he let his hand drop and turned away from me. 'Mister,' he said to the watch master, very slow, 'mister, this boy has gone weak in the head. Take him below. And send a couple of your men over to sculp them swiles on the ice.'

'The watch master looked at him for a minute, then he said, very quiet, 'You heard what the boy said, cap'n. No man of mine is going to kill them swiles. You had us killing swiles the three days since this boy was lost and you never gave a second thought to finding him till we came on him by accident. You're lucky you haven't the death of father and son on your conscience, if you have a conscience.'

"'I could have you flogged for that, mister,' said the cap'n. 'Do what you please, sir,' said the watch master and he took hold of me arm and led me below.

"I was real tired then and I just lay down on a bunk without a word to anyone. But when I was going off to sleep, I heard the engines turning over and I knew the Old Man had given up and left the swiles alive. We went back into St. John's then and I came back home. Because of what had happened, I was certain I'd not see a pennypiece of the crew's share for the catch. But a month went by and one day a man I'd never seen before came to the door of the house and gave me mother an envelope. Then he walked off without saying a word. When we opened the envelope, there was five hundred dollars in it in new banknotes. I hadn't told me mother about what happened out on the Front, and I didn't tell her then. It would've been too hard on her to think of me dad still out there on the ice. In those days a crew would be real lucky to get more'n a hundred dollars share a man, but I let her think we'd brought in an awful lot of pelts. We bought a share in a fishing boat with some of the money and I never went out on the ice since that day, nor wanted to. It's a cruel hard business out there, for man and beast, like I said."

"And Captain Kean," I said, "did he carry on sealing?"

"Oh, to be sure. He was a hard, proud man. I suppose sending me the money brought him some peace of mind. Anyway, he went out every season for another ten years and was the first captain ever to bring in a million pelts in his lifetime. They gave him some sort of medal for it and they gave him a place in the Assembly above in St. John's till he died. In his bed."

The old man paused to stare out at the driving shimmer of snowflakes. "Aye, in his bed," he went on quietly. "It's not for any of us to know for sure what happens in the hereafter, but if there's any justice in heaven, he'd have had to go out and face me dad and all the others he sent to their death on the Front. And that'd free them to go on to their rest and comfort. . . ."

He looked at me and, with a shrug, said, "But if only I could be certain Abram Kean's soul was out there in one of them whitecoats, I'd be out there killing swiles now."

3

Ménage à Trois

To have and to hold till death do us part.... Those words from the traditional marriage vow are often considered stuffy and old-fashioned these days, easily said and more easily forgotten. I'm sure they have never crossed the mind of my friend Nick Elgin. If they did, I think he'd find the irony of them hard to take.

Nick has never been the sort of person to contemplate a lasting relationship such as marriage. He has always loved women, of course, and many women have loved him, but the idea of settling down in a home with a particular woman was always unthinkable for him. Being free to move and to change wasn't just a matter of temperament; it was essential to his chosen profession. He's an architect and a renovator, and, during the first ten years I knew him, I can't recall him staying in one house more than six months. Invariably it would be an old rundown house in the downtown core of one Canadian city or another, and six months was usually the time it took him to renovate the building and sell it at a tidy profit.

It was through buying one of those renovated houses in Toronto that I got to know him. Like most writers, I need a permanent place in which to live and work and to house all the books and papers I've accumulated. But there is another side to me that yearns to be free of all those possessions and able to move at will to wherever I fancy; so I was attracted, perhaps enviously, to Nick Elgin and his vagrant way of life, and we became casual friends.

Friendship with Nick has to be casual. He's not much given to keeping in touch, but whenever he was passing through Toronto he'd call me and beg a bed for the night. At other times, I'd keep track of him through a network of mutual friends and could usually discover where he was holed up, gutting and redesigning yet another house. Whenever I had to pass through a city where he was working, I in turn would call him up and beg a bed for myself.

Without fail, whenever and wherever I bunked with him, I'd find him sharing his temporary roost with an attractive young woman, but always a different one. He's not unattractive, tall but inclined to put on weight, with a drooping mustache and dark tousled hair. There's a relaxed, easygoing style about him, and he always managed to be amusing, but I suspect that what most attracted women to him, initially at any rate, was the fact that he was usually unattached. He's in his early forties now, and the women invariably were at least fifteen years his junior. Each of them, I'm sure, harboured the futile illusion that she at last would induce him to settle down with her in whatever nest he happened to be refurbishing for someone else.

A philanderer, you say? No. To my knowledge, he never for a moment pretended to any of his women friends that he was not a bird of passage. While he was roosting, he was unfailingly attentive to the woman living with him, tender, generous, and faithful, because, oddly enough, he was not promiscuous and never involved himself with more than one woman at a time. In every relationship he intimated as gently as possible that it was a fleeting affair that would have to end when he moved on to his next project. I wouldn't want to suggest that all Nick's affairs were blissful. I can remember staying over with him several times when the tension between him and his current woman friend was all too evident, overshadowed by the approaching end of a house renovation and his inevitable departure. Yet somehow he managed to remain on good terms with quite a few of the women he had loved and left.

That, of course, is the way Nick Elgin used to live. At the moment he is still settled in the last house he renovated, two years ago, in Edmonton, and he earns a good if dull living by working on commission for local developers, designing plants and boring office towers for oil companies. And, to all appearances, he lives alone. I guess I'm the only one who knows that he is not really alone, but then I happen to have got caught in some of the strange events that ended his freedom and changed his life.

I was on my way back from the west coast then, where I'd been promoting one of my books. I was bored from autographing books in suburban bookstores and from shuttling from one radio station to another to answer the usual banal questions of talk-show hosts, and I decided it'd be fun to stop off and spend some time with Nick Elgin. I landed in Edmonton in the early evening and called him from the airport. I could tell from the conversation that he found my arrival somewhat inconvenient, but he offered me a bed for the night, a shade hesitantly, perhaps, and suggested that I meet him at a downtown restaurant for a drink and dinner before going on to his place.

When I arrived at The Railtown, an old but fashionable restaurant I'd eaten in before, he was already at a table. I sensed straight away that he was not his usual poised and casual self, and despite his welcoming smile and handshake, he seemed tense.

"On your own, Nick?" I asked when he'd ordered me a drink. "I'm amazed."

He seemed embarrassed. "Oh, no," he said quietly, "there is somebody, as usual. Elsa. She'll be along in a while."

He told me about the building he'd been renovating in one of the older sections of town, only a few blocks away. It was a three-storey brick building, which he converted to house a boutique on the ground floor, offices on the second, and a penthouse apartment on the top floor, in which he was living while the job was being finished, which wouldn't take long. My immediate guess was that this was one of those occasions when his woman friend had begun to resent his customary ending of such affairs.

"Look," I said, "if there's any problem with my staying over, just say so. I can easily get a room at a hotel."

He shook his head. "No problem," he said quickly. "Matter of fact, Elsa isn't staying with me at the moment, so there's plenty of room. I want you to stay over. It's been ages since we've had a chance to talk."

I asked him what he had in mind for his next job. He said he might take on several places he'd been offered in Vancouver, where there was the beginning of a real estate boom, but then added, rather gloomily, that he was beginning to get bored with renovations and might shop around in Toronto for something different.

A tall, slim young woman was shown to our table by the maitre d'. As I would have expected, she was pretty and young, with long dark hair, and stylishly dressed. Nick got up, kissed her cheek, and introduced her as Elsa Stein.

While Nick was ordering drinks, I studied her, and under the light from an overhead lamp I thought I could detect shadows of strain on her pale face. When I tried to start a conversation, she replied softly and shyly with a slight European accent. Not the type of woman Nick is usually attracted to, I thought. All the other women whom I'd met had been self-confident and vivacious.

Nick began a too obvious effort to enliven the conversation, with little success at first. I noticed that Elsa's hand shook whenever she raised her glass and that her eyes seemed almost glazed; either she'd been drinking before she arrived or she was slightly stoned on drugs.

During the dinner that followed, and the drinking of several bottles of wine, Elsa did become more lively and amusing, but there was an undercurrent of irritation to every exchange between her and Nick, which made me uncomfortable.

When coffee was served I excused myself and went to the washroom. As I approached the table on my return, I could see that the pair were having some sort of dispute. When I sat down I heard Nick say in a low voice, "It's just stupid. So you won't come back?" Elsa shook her head in reply.

There was an awkward silence for a few moments. Then, slurring the words, Elsa said, "So you'll be having a different kind of ménage à trois tonight?"

"Oh, cut out that crap, Elsa," Nick snapped at her.

She sat with tears brimming in her eyes for a moment, then grabbed her purse, got to her feet, and headed unsteadily toward the washrooms.

"I don't get this," I said. "Is it some sort of triangle situation?"

It's just nonsense," he said. "Elsa has this weird idea that my place is haunted."

"Well, is it?" I asked.

"You know what I think of that sort of crap," he said. "Elsa's a wonderful person. But she's neurotic as hell. It's been a mess here, and I'll be glad to get out of it."

He seemed so upset that I didn't feel inclined to say anything more on the subject. We sat in silence until Elsa returned. She seemed calmer but very pale. She said quietly to Nick, "I'm not feeling very well. Would you ask them to call me a taxi?"

"I'll see you home," Nick said.

"No," she said firmly, "I'll be all right. You stay and attend to your guest."

Nick shrugged and called the maitre d'. Conversation while we waited was uncomfortable, and I was relieved when a cab arrived and Nick escorted Elsa out.

When he returned he was so obviously upset that I suggested we settle the check and head for home. It was early October, clear and cold, and we walked the couple of blocks to his place in silence.

The renovated house was up to Nick's high standards, sandblasted and beautifully finished. The penthouse apartment seemed a perfect nest for an up-and-coming young oil executive, with studio windows reaching to the ceiling at the back and front and walls faced with light pine paneling. Appropriately sophisticated furniture, probably on loan from some local interior designer, was all in place.

The incident at the restaurant seemed to have depressed and exhausted Nick. He offered me a nightcap so half-heartedly that I refused, saying I felt tired. My room, a second bedroom, was in keeping with the perfect taste of the rest of the apartment, and there was a waterbed, something I'd always wanted to try. I didn't bother to close the shades over the tall window; I wanted to go to sleep under the clear sky brilliantly spangled with stars.

Actually I was quite tired. The boredom of promotion tours is always exhausting. I was drifting quickly and pleasantly into sleep when, suddenly, I found myself alert again. I was not alone. A figure, certainly a woman's figure, stood over the bed, between me and the window. Elsa, I thought. But no, it wasn't Elsa. The light of the stars shone brightly, not just through the diaphanous gown she wore but through her body and long hair. A dream, I told myself, a dream. . . .

The waterbed undulated as someone slid in under the duvet beside me. Warm hands sensually and gently ran over my shoulders and chest, then slid down toward my thighs. I tried to respond. But there was nothing there for my arms to enfold, my hands to stroke. The caresses continued, marvelous and expert. I was being made love to by a woman without being able to participate. The pleasure was more intense than any I had ever known, and I was aroused almost to the point of agony, before the storm of climax came and was suddenly over. I drifted off into oblivion.

I had no sense of time. Suddenly I was awake again, as sometimes happens when you make love and slide into sleep, but I was alone in the waterbed. The sky beyond the tall window was still jet black and studded with cold stars, and now I was terrified. I sat up and switched on a bedside lamp.

With its fresh paint, its contemporary furniture, and its hanging plants, the room looked an unlikely place for a haunting. I felt slightly reassured. Vivid though the experience had seemed, it had to have been a dream. But I knew I was not going to be able to sleep again, so I got up, put on a robe, and sat in an easy chair by the window, glancing through a magazine and smoking.

A few minutes later there was a gentle tap on the door. I called out and Nick stepped in, also in a robe, carrying two glasses of cognac. He gave me one and sat down on the edge of the bed.

"Saw your light on, so I thoght I'd give you that nightcap. Couldn't sleep?"

"No," I said, "Had a weird dream."

He nodded. "People do here. I wondered if Alice would bother you."

"What do you mean?" I asked. "Who's Alice?"

He sighed. "My resident ghost. I should have warned you, but I wanted to find something out. What was your dream?"

I told him about the woman who had appeared and what had happened. He listened with an odd smile growing on his face.

"She's good, isn't she?" he said when I'd finished. "A credit to her profession. I guess she's trying to make me jealous."

He studied my bewildered expression for a few moments. Then he told me that as soon as he had moved into the apartment, six months before, he had the feeling that he was never quite alone. Whenever he turned around, he got the impression that someone had been watching him and had just ducked out of sight. Sometimes he would just catch the sound of light footsteps, a woman's footsteps, and occasionally a gentle laugh.

"To tell you the truth," he said, "I thought I was losing my mind. I was working my ass off at the time, finishing another house across town and trying to keep the downstairs renovations moving here. Then one day when I was here alone, when I'd been hearing those footsteps and that giggle, I suddenly said on impulse, out loud, 'Alice, this is my place. If you want to hang around, at least make yourself useful.'"

"How did you know her name was Alice?" I asked.

"I didn't," Nick said. "The name and what I said just came into my mind. But it worked. Within a few days I began to notice odd things happening around the place. For instance, because I was so busy I used to forget to water the houseplants. When I went to water them, I found they'd already been watered. At night I'd find my bed made up, although I never bothered to do that myself. If I left used glasses on the kitchen counter, I'd find them washed and polished. Ashtrays would be emptied and cleaned — all the little chores a woman is inclined to do around an apartment."

"And did that convince you? I asked.

"At first it just convinced me that I was going crazy." he said, "and for the first time in my life I seriously thought of going to a shrink. But then one day I had lunch with Jake Leonard. . . ."

"Who's he?" I asked.

"Oh, he's in real estate," Nick said. "The guy who handled the sale of this place. Matter of fact, he's Elsa's boss. We've known each other for a long time. Anyway, he asked me how I was liking this place. I said it was fine but that the vibes were a bit strange. He laughed and said that he would have thought I'd appreciate the vibes here. Then he told me that ten years before I bought this place, it had been used as a halfway house for wayward girls — hookers, for the most part. I had to laugh, but for some reason I didn't tell him what had been happening to me here."

"All this was before Elsa?" I asked.

He nodded and said, "Yes. Of course I was attracted to her the moment I saw her. She's a sexy, beautiful woman. But I hadn't made any move, even though I could see she liked me. But I'm, coming to that. That night, after I'd had lunch with Jake, I was in bed and I had a visitation, or dream, or whatever, just like the one you've just had. And the night after that, and the next night again. . . ."

"Sounds gruelling," I kidded, "and very gratifying."

He didn't laugh.

"No, it wasn't," he said. "It was a pleasant experience, as you know now. But only once. You know me — I like sex, but I'm not a passive type. I've never much liked being made love to. I really like making love with a woman, and with . . . with Alice, there was nobody there. I knew I couldn't take it night after night, dream or not, without cracking up. So that's why I finally started things going with Elsa."

He got to his feet and walked over to stare out the window at the sky, which was now a pale silver.

"Did you tell her what had been happening?" I asked.

"No way," Nick said. "After all, I wasn't sure I hadn't been imagining everything. I didn't want her to think I was crazy. She was a bit dubious about me at first anyway. Probably she'd heard something about my past with women from Jake Leonard or someone else in the business. We'd had lunch and two dinner dates before she agreed to come up here for a drink one night. She seemed very tense, had one drink, and then insisted on going home. Much later, she told me she'd disliked the atmosphere in this place from the moment she'd first set foot in it."

"And Alice," I said, "how did she react?"

"She didn't appear, but in the middle of the night a framed poster that was hanging in my bedroom fell off the wall and smashed. I should have taken the warning more seriously than I did. As a matter of fact, there was no sign of Alice for a whole week, and I began to believe that it had all been in my imagination."

Nick sat down on the edge of the bed, rubbing his eyes.

"At the end of the week," he went on, "I took Elsa out to dinner again. I was feeling really good, and we had a great time and drank a lot. We came back here and went to bed together. I don't know how long it was after we'd fallen asleep, but I was awakened by the sound of Elsa gasping and sobbing. You may have noticed in my bedroom that there are french doors opening out onto the sundeck. Well, Elsa was spread-eagled against them struggling and crying as though she was trying to force her body through the doors. I jumped up and grabbed her, and she fainted in my arms. I laid her down on the bed, and after a few moments she came to. She was wet with perspiration and shivering and she began sobbing again. It was quite a while before she could tell me what happened. She said she'd had a nightmare, that she'd felt herself dragged out of bed, flung across the room, and pressed so hard against the doors that she couldn't break free. I put a blanket over her and gradually calmed her down. When she felt better, she insisted that I take her home to her apartment. And I stayed with her there that night."

Nick got up and stared out the window again. He didn't say anything for several minutes.

Eventually he said in a quiet voice, "I know you'll think it rotten of me, but I didn't tell her anything about what had been happening to me. I convinced myself that it would terrify her even more. Maybe I was too embarrassed to tell her about Alice in bed with me. Or maybe just too selfish. Later that morning at her place, when she felt calm enough to talk about it again, she said she was certain my place was haunted, that something dreadful must have happened there, and that she'd never go back there again. It was too late for me to admit anything then, so I insisted that it must have been just a nightmare and that she must have walked in her sleep. She still insists that this is an evil place and that it's haunted."

"But last night in the restaurant she mentioned something about a ménage à trois," I said. "Does that mean you've told her about Alice since?"

Nick looked more embarrassed than ever.

"In a way, I have," he said with a shrug. "Ever since, whenever we're together, it's at her place. She won't come here. And to try to ease the situation I've made a sort of joke of it, saying that I'm having a really wild time with a ghost here and telling her that she should come and join us. As you must have guessed last night, the kidding didn't work."

"And Alice," I said, "have you been having a wild time with her here?"

He shook his head. "No, not a trace of her, no visits in the night since Elsa was here. Not until tonight, that is. And what happened to you confirms what I should have admitted months ago — that it's not imagination. The place really is haunted."

I suddenly noticed that it was almost seven o'clock, and I had to catch an early flight to Regina, the next stop in my promotion tour. Nick made us some coffee while I got ready and then drove me to the airport.

Nick was silent most of the way, but when we were nearly there he said, "When the house is sold and I move on, I suppose I can put it all behind me. But I am worried about Elsa. She really is a sweet kid, but very insecure and intense. And somehow what happened seems to have made her very dependent on me. I just don't know what I can do."

He didn't say anything more, and, good friends though we had always been, I couldn't think of anything appropriate to say. He didn't need to be reminded that he'd behaved badly and that his affair with Elsa was going to end more painfully than the others. For once I was relieved to say good-bye to him and board my plane.

I didn't hear from Nick, and hardly expected to. I imagined that he had sold the property in Edmonton and moved on, possibly to Vancouver. For a month or two after getting back to Toronto, I thought a lot about what had happened in that apartment. But then I got absorbed in work on another book and the experience faded to the back of my mind. I came to the conclusion that somehow Nick and I had shared some sort of erotic hallucination, maybe telepathically. I was surprised when, about six months later, a friend of Nick's mentioned that he was still living in Edmonton and working on a big corporate project. It struck me as possible that for once he hadn't behaved selfishly and had stayed on because of Elsa. I was glad. The friend didn't know if Nick was still living in the building he'd renovated, and I smiled to myself at the thought of someone else inheriting Alice and her seductive ways.

There was no opportunity for me to go out west again, but one day a few months later I noticed in the paper that there was to be a big architectural conference in town, and Nick was listed as a speaker in a panel on urban renewal. I hoped that he would call me as usual, but when he didn't, I left a message for him at the hotel where the conference was being held.

He called me later that day, sounding harassed, and apologized for not getting in touch. He asked me if I could meet him for a drink late that evening, because he had to get back to Edmonton the following morning and we arranged a time and place.

There weren't many people in the hotel lobby, but I didn't recognize him at first. Wearing a tuxedo, he looked smart, but surprisingly thinner and older; there were streaks of grey in his hair that I'd never noticed before. Although he was standing facing in my direction, he seemed not to notice me until I walked up to him. But he seemed very glad to see me and shook my hand with an odd intensity, and thanked me for helping him escape the after-dinner speeches at the conference banquet. He led the way to a quiet lounge across the lobby and we ordered drinks.

"So you're still in Edmonton?" I said.

"Yes, I am," he said with a heavy sigh. "I really didn't have any choice."

"Because of Elsa?" I asked.

He stared at me, obviously astounded, with his hands clenched over the arms of his chair. "You mean you haven't heard what happened?" he said.

I shook my head; I had no idea what he meant. Still staring at me, he slumped back in his seat. Even in the dim light of the lounge, his face looked extraordinarily pale and worn, like the face of someone struggling to emerge from a personal crisis or a serious illness.

"Well," he said after a long pause, "when you left after that visit last year, I just didn't know what to do about that situation. For a couple of months I spent more time with Elsa in her apartment than I did in my own place. Elsa was very happy about that, of course. But I wasn't too happy, because I knew I was going to have to pull out."

"And the . . . the ghost?" I put in. "Alice, I mean. Any more visits?"

"She didn't reappear," he said, "but she made her presence known, all right. Whenever I spent a few nights at Elsa's, I'd come back to my place and find a mess. Hanging plants torn down and scattered on the floor, glasses and plates smashed in the kitchen. But whenever I slept at my place, the next morning the plants would be watered, the glasses would be washed and polished. But no, there were no visitations at night."

He reached for his drink and the ice cubes tinkled as he took a deep gulp. I'd never seen him in such bad shape. He gave another deep sigh.

"If only I'd done something sooner," he said sadly. "As it happened, a developer I know in Vancouver called me and said he had a deal for me. I flew down to meet him and we discussed the project for a couple of days. It wasn't the greatest deal, but I wanted it anyway, and I'd more or less decided to ask Elsa to move out to Vancouver with me. Then there was a message waiting for me from Jake Leonard, asking me to call him at once. He told me there'd been a dreadful accident and that Elsa was dead. He didn't tell me what had happened, and I didn't ask because somehow I knew what whatever had happened would be my fault. He said I'd better come back on the next flight.

"Jake was at the airport with a cop, a detective-sergeant, who said he'd like to interview me right away. There was to be an inquest the following day. On the way to police headquarters, the cop told me, as sympathetically as he could, what had happened.

"Apparently, because there'd been a lot of burglaries in the neighbourhood, Jake had asked Elsa to check out my apartment on her lunch hour. Even though she hated the place, she said she would. Probably because she . . . well, wanted to please me . . . Oh, God . . ."

Nick couldn't go on and sat for several minutes with his face in his hands.

"Later that afternoon," he said at last, "a neighbour saw Elsa lying on the patio behind the house. She was dead. She'd fallen from the sundeck outside my bedroom. When the police examined the apartment they found those french doors in my room smashed open."

Nick stared at me, his face paler and more agonized than ever, and said slowly, "I don't have to tell you what passed through my mind. The cops told me that at first they thought that Elsa might have surprised an intruder and been pushed off the sundeck. But they hadn't been able to find any sign of a break-in. So that's why they were anxious to talk with me.

"When we got to police headquarters, I told the sergeant about my relationship with Elsa. He was a decent enough guy, but you know cops, they're so conventional. He made it obvious that he thought it sort of sleazy for someone of my age to have been having an affair with someone as young as Elsa. I didn't tell him anything about Alice and that side of things, of course. Who'd have believed me? So I signed a formal statement. And then this cop leaned over and said to me, "Y'know, there's one thing that's really weird about this case. About ten years ago that place was used as a halfway house for girls, delinquents. I was with the vice squad then, and I hauled in a runaway kid from a small town up north, name of Alice Switton. She was fined for soliciting, put on probation, and placed in that house. Couple of days later, she threw herself out of a third-storey window and died on the exact spot where your friend died.

Nick took another deep drink and stared at the floor.

"I don't know how I didn't break down and tell him everything," he said. "Or at the inquest, when I had to go over the whole thing again. The jury, after a lot of hassle and delay, came down with a verdict of death by misadventure. And then there was Elsa's funeral."

The effort of telling what had happened seemed to have exhausted him. It struck me that he looked like a ghost himself. For want of anything better to say, I asked, "So where are you living now?"

He looked up with an odd smile, as though puzzled by the question.

"Why, there, of course." he said, "in the apartment. Where else would I go?"

"But, Nick," I said, "it's obvious that all that was a helluva strain for you. Wouldn't you be better to move, put all that behind you?"

He shook his head slowly. "How could I?" he said. "They're my responsibility now, Alice as much as Elsa. And they always will be. They'd be with me no matter where I went. And besides, we get along together very well."

The resigned way in which he spoke shocked me as much as what he had said.

"But, Nick," I said, knowing it was pointless, "you . . . you should get some help. . . ."

"What help do I need?" he said with an edge of impatience in his voice. "They look after me. In every way you could imagine. And they always will, I guess."

He stood up suddenly, patted me on the shoulder, and murmured, "Don't worry about me." Then he turned and walked away.

When occasionally I run into other friends of Nick Elgin, I ask them if they've had news of him. Very few of them have been in touch with him. He's still living in Edmonton. One friend who had run into him in the street there remarked to me, "He seems to keep very much to himself these days," and I had a strange impulse to laugh out loud. But I didn't. No one else would understand.

4

The Forbidden Ground

Bill W., as I'll have to call him, since he asked me not to use his real name, is an ex-Mountie. And looks it, every solid inch of his heavy six-foot body. He took early retirement from the force when he was sixty and he now works part-time in the administration of a security company. The rest of the time he potters around the neat bungalow he bought in Etobicoke with his savings, making its narrow garden the envy of the street.

He strikes you as a very private and imperturbable man, nodding to neighbours as they pass rather than smiling or greeting them. That came, I guess, from a working life that required him to be watchful and to hold himself apart from other people. But since he was my next-door neighbour, it was nearly impossible for us not to get to know each other. We'd exchange a few words whenever we were out in our backyards or when we were shoveling our driveways in winter. I soon found him to be a shy, rather sensitive man who wanted to be friendly but had to struggle at it. His wife and mine were on much easier terms and regularly exchanged gossip, recipes, and cups of sugar.

Bill had never talked to me very much about his life in the Mounties. Not until that night last August. It had been hot and sticky for a week and we were due for one of those late summer thunderstorms. Dusk seemed to come on suddenly, with that eerie green light you get before a storm, so I stepped out back to have a look at the sky. Bill was at his back door, doing the same thing.

"Looks like it'll be a good one," he said, nodding toward a bulging front of black clouds to the west.

"We need it," I said, "ground's parched."

At that moment, lightning lit up the sky, and a few fat raindrops splattered on the driveway.

"I'm parched myself," he said. "Want to come in and have a beer?"

"Sure. Love to. Thanks."

I stepped over the low fence, and he held open the door to his screened-in back porch.

"Have a seat here," he said, "it'll be cooler," and he went on into his kitchen. There was a long roll of thunder, but the rain was still holding off. Bill returned and handed me a long cool beer.

"Mary's off in Manitoba, visiting family." he muttered. "Good thing, too. She can't abide storms."

We sat in silence for several minutes, sipping our beers and gazing out at the dim garden, which looked, in the green light, as though it were at the bottom of an ocean.

"It looks so weird out there," I said finally, "so ghostly. . . ."

There was a crackling flash of lightning, followed in seconds by a blast of thunder, and then the rain lashed down all around us.

"Do you believe in ghosts, then?" Bill asked, so softly that I could barely hear him against the hiss of rain.

"Well, I sort of collect ghost stories," I said, "even though I've never encountered a ghost myself. What about you?"

He turned to me and said slowly, "Same as you. I'd never actually seen a ghost. Thought it was a lot of nonsense. . . ." More lightning and another thunderous crash interrupted him. "Until the last year I was in the force, when I was stationed up in The Pas."

"Why don't you tell me about it?"

He paused for a minute or two, as though he was having second thoughts about it, then shrugged and began.

"The Pas was where they sent me when they knew I was going to take early retirement. Mary — she's from Manitoba — hadn't liked Regina, where I'd been before, but we both liked The Pas. It's still kind of a last frontier, the sort of place where the Mounties have always amounted to something. There's still a lot of characters, trappers, guides, lone-dog prospectors, and because of the size of the place, you got to know most of them, so you could iron out any problems before they got too serious. That's how I got to know Norm Duncan, only the problem there wasn't him but his son, Dave. Norm was a real decent guy; he'd lived in and around The Pas all his life, and worked as a trapper in the winter, a tourist guide and handyman in the summer. But the boy was something else. A drifter, big and ugly and mean. He'd sign on for logging and construction jobs and be gone for a few months. Then he'd show up in town and booze away whatever he'd earned. And he'd always get himself into fights. Because I respected his dad, I'd do what I could for him, put him in the cooler and, if he had to go up before the magistrate, put in a good word for him and get him off on probation."

The storm had passed and the rain had stopped. It was cool and so quiet that it seemed we were in the countryside rather than sitting in a suburban house.

"But finally," Bill went on, "he really got himself into trouble. Nearly killed an Indian in a fight and got himself three months in the pen. When he got back to town, on probation, it was late fall and I was expecting trouble. But somehow Norm persuaded the boy to go trapping with him for the winter. That year Norm had leased a cabin and a couple of good trap lines down near Deer Lake from an old trapper. I helped them load up their canoe, and I can tell you I was glad to see them set off, because I knew Dave wouldn't be able to come out of there till spring break-up."

Bill fetched us another couple of beers.

It didn't occur to me that he'd never come out," he said as he sat down again. "It was late in May when Norm Duncan showed up at the post, asking for me. The moment I saw him I knew something was up, so I took him to a café across the street for coffee. He went down to a booth near the back, where we wouldn't be overheard.

"'Well, Norm,' I said to him, 'how did the trapping go?' 'Best season I ever had, Bill,' he said. 'We'll make a bundle.' But he didn't look very happy about it, and he just sat there across from me, staring into his coffee cup. 'Well, is there some problem, Norm?' I asked. He raised his eyes from his cup, looked at me silently for a few seconds, and finally said, 'I don't know how to say this, Bill, but there's something strange about that place. You'll have to hear me out.'

'Norm told me they'd had an easy enough trip out to the trapping area. The cabin, still in good shape, was just east of a loop in the Saskatchewan River. One trap line ran around the loop close to the river, and the other, a longer line, lay to the southeast. It had snowed a bit before they arrived, and there was a heavy fall the day they got there that covered the ground.'

"He sent Dave off to set traps around the river line, while he worked the traps along the southern line. A couple of days later, they each went out to check the traps they'd set. Norm picked up half-a-dozen pelts on his line, but when he got back to the cabin Dave was already there, empty-handed and sullen. The boy told him he'd found plenty of animal tracks but that every one of the traps he'd set had been sprung but was empty. There were no human tracks in the snow, but he was certain that somehow the traps had been robbed. He said he'd seen smoke coming out of the bush across the river from the loop, so he figured there must be a trapper over there who was poaching their trap line."

"Dave told his father he was going across the river to have it out with whoever was over there. Although Norm didn't believe the traps had been robbed, he decided to go along to make sure there was no trouble. The river hadn't frozen yet, so they were able to paddle downstream around the loop to near where Dave said he'd seen the smoke. They climbed the bank into the bush and, sure enough, there was a small tumbledown cabin there. When they knocked on the door, it opened slowly and an Indian, a very old man, stood there. Dave accused him straight off of having robbed their trap line. But the old man just shook his head. 'I would never go on that land,' he said. 'I would not hunt there because that is sacred ground. Many of my people from many years ago are buried there and their spirits guard that place. You will never trap animals there because the spirits will not allow it.'

"According to Norm, Dave yelled at the old man that he was a liar and a thief, and would have hit him if Norm hadn't stepped between them. The old man seemed unafraid and quietly said, 'If you are wise and respect that ground, the spirits will reward you and your trapping in other places will be good.' Then he went back into his cabin and closed the door on them. Norm had a job convincing the boy to leave it at that and go back across to their own cabin. And he had an even harder job convincing him to stay off the Indian ground. Dave was convinced that the Indian had told them that story so that he could trap that land himself, and for a couple of weeks he just sat brooding in the cabin, refusing to help his father. But sure enough, as the old Indian had said, the trapping on the southern line got better and better. In only a month Norm had taken more pelts than he'd ever trapped before in a whole winter season. In the end, although he still argued that they were being tricked. Dave had to give him a hand in stretching and scraping the pelts just to keep up with them. And all the time he kept a watch on the ground beside the river, certain he would spot the Indian trapping there. But he never did."

It was getting late now, and there were very few lights in the neighbouring houses, but I didn't mention the time. I wanted to hear out the story that had so absorbed Bill that he'd hardly touched his beer.

"Break-up was early that spring," Bill went on, "but to get upstream to The Pas from where Norm and his son were they had to wait till the run-off eased a bit. They had so many pelts by that time Norm wondered if they'd both be able to fit in the boat. But when the time came for them to leave, Dave told his father he was going to stay on in the cabin. He said he didn't want to go back to town, where he'd just get into trouble, so he was going to hunt and fish for a few weeks more. Then, when the ground was drier, he'd walk out to the nearest highway and hitch back to The Pas. Norm wasn't too happy about leaving the boy out there, but he knew there was a good possibility Dave'd get into more trouble in town. Norm was also worried that when he had gone the boy would try to work out his grudge against the old man across the river. But it seemed there was little use arguing with him — Dave was dead set on staying. Before he left, Norm warned him to stay away from the Indian and to keep out of the burial ground. All the way back up the river to The Pas he'd worried about Dave and what had happened, and that's why he came to see me."

At last Bill paused and took a gulp of his beer. He glanced over at me and shrugged.

"Well, what was I to say to him? I'd heard a lot of stuff about Indian spirits and burial grounds. Who hasn't? But I never took much account of it. And I have to admit I was relieved to hear that Dave wasn't back in town. At least out there he couldn't get his hands on any booze, and maybe a month on his own'd drive some sense into him. So I just said to Norm that the boy was used to fending for himself and would probably be all right out there.

"Norm did make a bundle of money on his pelts, and for the next month or so he stayed around town. He didn't take on his usual job as a tourist guide, perhaps because he didn't need the money, but more likely because he wanted to be around when Dave showed up in town. Whenever I saw him I'd ask if the boy had returned, and he'd just shake his head. As the weeks went by I could see he was getting more and more worried. Once I suggested to him that maybe Dave had taken off on some job and not bothered to come back to town, but I could see he wasn't convinced. Finally, in the middle of July, he came to see me and said he was going to head down the river in the morning and see how Dave was making out. He tried to make a joke about Dave not needing him because he had all those Indian spirits for neighbours, but I could see that he was afraid something bad had happened. I asked him to bring me back some fish, and he said he would."

Bill stopped and just sat looking down at his feet for a couple of minutes. Then he said very quietly, "What I'm going to tell you now is just between ourselves, eh? It's something I've never told anyone else. In fact, all I've told you so far about what happened out at Norm's cabin, I'd kept to myself. I didn't report it to my super or talk about it to any of the guys in the force at The Pas because . . . well, I dunno, I didn't want them getting a big laugh over Norm Duncan and the Indian spirits. But a couple of months passed without Norm or the boy showing up, and then I was really in an awkward spot. In the end I went to my super and told him that I thought Duncan might have run into trouble. All I said was that Norm had gone down the river in July to pick up Dave at their cabin near Deer Lake and they hadn't come back. It wasn't any big deal in those parts for guys to be away hunting for a month, but two months was a long time. I suggested that maybe I should go out to the cabin and take a look, and the super agreed. There were half-a-dozen charter pilots with float planes at The Pas, so I got one of them I knew to fly me down to a lake about five miles short of Norm's cabin. When he dropped me off, I told him to come back and pick me up in a couple of days.

"It's rocky ground thereabouts, so the bush isn't that thick, and it didn't take me long to work my way across to the cabin. As I came down the slope toward it, I spotted Norm's boat pulled up on the bank farther down, and it was still loaded. I yelled out a couple of times as I got near the cabin, but nobody answered. When I reached the cabin, the door was half-open. I stepped inside and could see right away that nobody had been in there for quite a while. Dust and leaves had blown in and some animal had been gnawing at the food locker. I went outside and called Norm's name a couple times more. I knew I was wasting my breath, but it helped calm me down. I just didn't like the feel of being alone in that place. Then I went and looked at Norm's boat. It looked as though it hadn't been touched since it had been pulled up on the bank. There was a lot of rust on Norm's rifle and shotgun, and animals had been into the supplies there, too. I sat and thought about it for a while, trying to imagine what had happened. Then I remembered what Norm had said about the old Indian in a cabin across the river. On the off chance that he might still be there, I decided to go over.

"I pushed the boat back into the water and got in. The outboard wouldn't start, so I just let the current carry me downstream and guided the boat with a paddle. I kept an eye on the far bank, hoping I'd see a trail, but I couldn't see anything, so when I was halfway around the loop of the river, I paddled in and hauled up the boat on a sandbar. The bank was rocky, but not very high or steep, so I had no problem getting up. I was in luck, because a hundred yards farther along the bank I could see a cabin through the trees. But when I reached it there was only the remnants of what had once been a cabin. The walls were still standing, but they were rotten, and what remained of the roof must have collapsed under the weight of snow years and years before. Nobody could have been living there during the past winter. I thought maybe I'd found the wrong place, so I worked my way along the bank all the way around the loop in both directions. Not a sign that there'd ever been another cabin or human being there. The going wasn't hard and the weather wasn't hot, but I was sweating when I got back down to the boat. I don't scare easily, but something was scaring me real bad then, and I had a hard time getting a grip on myself. Maybe because I knew I'd have to search that area across the river where Norm's first trap line had been. After what Norm had told me, I had no choice. And I knew in my bones that I was going to find something terrible.

"I looked across at the place. The land inside the river loop was shaped like a dome, not very high. There must have been a fire a while back because the timber, pine and birch, was young and well spaced out, with not too much underbrush because it was rocky.

"There was nothing for it but to go over there, so I paddled the boat across and beached it. I looked around in it for an axe, but there wasn't one. Then it occurred to me that if Norm had arrived and found the cabin empty, he'd have set off in search of his boy and he'd have taken an axe with him, to blaze a trail. I set off, making for the high ground and taking my time, but I was still sweating. I saw a few blazes on the trees, probably marking Norm's trap line, but I didn't follow them because I knew I'd get a better view from the high ground.

"When I got up there, I didn't see anything at first. Then I spotted something that just didn't fit. About two hundred yards down the back slope, there was a birch sapling with its branches stripped and something red dangling from it. There was a steep bluff immediately below me, so I had to find a place where I could climb down. When I got down to level ground, I was only thirty yards from the birch sapling, but even from there I couldn't quite make out what was hanging from it. But I suppose deep down I really knew what it was, and as I drew closer I hadn't any doubt. It was the remains of a human body, strung to the top of the sapling, but now nothing left of it but a few bones tangled in rags of clothing. The red I'd seen was the remains of a red checked shirt that I'd seen Dave wearing when he set off, and I knew why it was dangling up there. He'd been caught in an Indian snare. An old Indian trapper had explained to me once how they used saplings and rawhide to snare animals in the old days. As I came forward, staring up and sick to my stomach, I stumbled on something. It was part of an old hunting boot, slashed clear through the instep. And then I saw something else. Around the foot of the sapling bones and shreds of clothing were scattered and there were two skulls. One I knew would be Dave's, and the other, because I recognized a cap lying beside it, must have been Norm Duncan's. I walked away to sit on a rock and smoke a cigarette, trying not to look at the sapling or even to think about it. I had a hard job just forcing myself not to get up and run away.

"In the end I managed to calm myself down and I walked over to the tree again. There was a rusted shotgun and a rusted axe lying among the bones. And there were a couple of cuts in the trunk of the birch. It was obvious what had happened. As soon as his father left, Dave had gone down there where he wasn't meant to go after some game, and got snared. He just died hanging upside down there. When Norm came back and found the cabin empty, he knew exactly where to look for Dave, because he knew how stubborn and headstrong that boy was. When he saw the body, he started hacking at the tree and somehow slashed his foot off. Bled to death."

Bill fell silent again, wearily rubbing his forehead with his hand. I didn't say anything.

"So what was there to do?" he finally went on in a subdued voice. "Only an Indian would have set the snare for Dave. But what Indian? I knew there'd never been an Indian across the river, and I knew the nearest band was a hundred miles away, with far better hunting on their reserve. I suppose I could have gone back and reported what I'd found, and then there'd have been all the palaver of an investigation and an inquest. But what good would that have done? What verdict would they have arrived at? Who would they blame? Murder by spirits unknown?"

"So what did you do, Bill?" I asked quietly.

"Well, it was getting on for dusk," he said, "so I just cut Dave's remains down. It wasn't hard — the rawhide was so dried up and brittle. Then I went back down to the boat. There were some cans of food in an old ammunition box, and I built a fire and a lean-to. I ate a bit, and tried to sleep but I just couldn't. At first light, I took a shovel from the boat and went up and buried what was left of Dave and Norm, making sure no one would ever find traces of the grave. Then I took down the shovel, the shotgun, and the axe and put them in the boat. I kept back a couple of cans of beans and I pushed the boat out into the stream.

"I didn't go back near the cabin. Just made my way around to the lake and waited there till the plane picked me up the next morning. I told the pilot I'd found the cabin empty and nobody around, and I asked him to fly a few passes low over the area. He spotted the boat, overturned below some rapids downstream. There was nowhere to land nearby, so we headed back to The Pas. There was a bit of an investigation, and they decided that the Duncans must have gone over the rapids by accident, overturned and drowned. There were no next-of-kin. A few months later I took my retirement and moved down here."

"Do you believe in ghosts now?" I asked.

"I suppose, considering all the evidence, I have to," he said slowly.

5

In Death As In Life

Death is the dividing line between doctors and people like me, who are interested in ghosts, but the division is not always clear. A case in point was provided by Jack Ludlow, who until a few years ago was my family doctor and who, at the same time, was a close neighbour in the Toronto suburb where we lived. Since I've always been inexplicably healthy, I never gave him much business, but we were friends nevertheless. We somehow managed to get together for dinner at least once a month. Because he was a bachelor and a workaholic, he usually took my wife and me out to one of his favourite restaurants; and because I was a perpetually hard-up writer, we in turn would invite him to our place to eat. It really didn't matter much where we ate: although he and I both enjoyed good food and drink, what we most enjoyed was talking late into the night. My wife enjoyed the talk too, up to a point, but she also liked to get to bed at a reasonable time, so we were usually left alone at the table to talk as long as possible about whatever took our fancy.

One such night, not unexpectedly, we got around to arguing about death, or rather our different attitudes toward it. He'd made some crack about my fascination with the afterlife, and I accused him, and all doctors, of having a boringly limited view of life. "All of you," I said, "assume that when the body's engine cuts out, that's the end of it. You hand the body over to an undertaker and forget about it. You never stop to think what happens to the life that was in that body when you were tinkering with it."

Jack was a lanky, untidy man, always restless with energy, but as I made that last remark, he became unusually still and thoughtful. He looked down at his coffee cup as he rotated it in its saucer and said quietly, "What you say is true enough, but only because we have to take that attitude to survive. As I hardly need tell you, doctoring is tough enough under ordinary circumstances, and far too many of us become alcoholics or junkies. Once a doctor starts involving himself with the hereafter, he's almost certain to crack up. I did once, quite a few years ago, and it almost finished me. It took me years to recover from it."

He met the curious glance I threw at him but said nothing more.

"I never would have guessed that about you, Jack," I said. "Can you tell me about it?"

He continued to stare at me, as though he was wondering whether he could trust me by revealing something that had obviously affected him very deeply.

"The difference between life and death," he said slowly, "is an obsession with doctors. After all, a minor error of judgment can wipe out a life, and can't ever be corrected. So when the distinction between life and death becomes blurred, the effect can be traumatic. It certainly was for me.

"This happened seven years ago. I had a call one morning from a Dr. Ralph Mooney. He'd been one of my professors at medical school and also served on the disciplinary board of the College of Physicians. I was surprised to hear from him. I hadn't been one of his better students and was now only a lowly family doctor. He wanted to know if I'd been in touch with Jeff Aitken lately. Aitken had been a close friend of mine at school and a brilliant student. He'd gone on after graduate school to become one of the best brain surgeons in Ontario and perhaps in the country. And because he was in such demand, we rarely saw each other anymore. So I said no, I hadn't seen him in more than two years. Mooney, obviously embarrassed, said, "You may not know this, but I'm Jeff's legal guardian. I'm afraid he's been having some problems lately, and, because I know you've been close to him, closer than I ever have, I thought that maybe you could help. Could we meet and discuss this? Fairly soon?

"Mooney is a nice man, but too formal to discuss anything confidential over the phone, so I agreed to meet him at the Faculty Club late the following afternoon. I was puzzled. I had heard that Jeff's marriage had broken up for much the same reason our friendship had lapsed — because he worked incessantly. By all accounts the divorce had been messy and expensive, but I knew that Mooney wouldn't have approached me about that. When we met he came to the point at once in the same dry, precise way he delivered lectures. It appeared that the College of Physicians had recently received two complaints against Jeff from former patients, which the board would have to examine, and that a suit of malpractice had already been filed against him. Hospital colleagues had admitted confidentially that they had noticed a decline in his work since his divorce. They suggested drink might be one cause of this, but so far nobody had dared to broach that problem with him. At the moment he was on a voluntary leave of absence.

"To that Mooney added that perhaps another part of Aitken's problem might arise from the fact that since his divorce he had been living alone in a remote house north of Toronto that he'd inherited from his father.

'That's no place at all,' Mooney said, 'for a man suffering the kind of stress that divorce so often causes. That family has suffered too much already in the cause of medicine, and the last thing we want to see is a fine career ruined. So we wondered if you could resume your friendship without any embarrassment and find out what can be done before . . . things get out of control.'

"I suspected that after so many years of living very different kinds of lives, Jeff and I might find ourselves very far apart. But I was a little flattered by Mooney's approach, and I was concerned by what he'd told me, so I agreed to try.

"That evening I tried to call Jeff. Only his former home downtown was listed in the directory. I didn't want to talk to his ex-wife, so I had to ask the operator for his new number. There was no answer when I dialled it, and there was no answering service, which was odd for a doctor as busy as Jeff must have been. I tried again the following morning and again in the afternoon. Still no reply. I wondered if he'd gone out of town to escape his problems. Ralph Mooney had said he didn't think so, and a colleague of Jeff's at the hospital, whom I knew, said she was certain that he was still in town.

"The next morning I tried the number again and let it ring for several minutes. Suddenly the phone was knocked off its cradle with a clatter. There was a long silence, and finally a voice said indistinctly, 'What?'

"I said, 'Jeff, it's Jack . . . Jack Ludlow.'

"There was another long silence, then he said, 'Ludlow . . . Jack Ludlow . . . Oh, yes . . . Jack, hi! . . .'

"I could tell that it wasn't just sleepiness affecting him but either drink or drugs, and that's disturbing in a profession that sees the worst effects of both.

"As casually as I could, I said, 'Long time since we've been in touch, Jeff. Thought it'd be fun to get together.'

"Another long pause. 'That's very true,' he said, 'a long time. Haven't been too well, but we should meet for a drink . . . Maybe . . . maybe you'd like to drop out here sometime?'

"'Sure,' I said, 'I've been wanting to see this ancestral estate of yours. When should I come?'

"'Not much of a place at present, but beggars can't be choosers. You heard about the divorce?'

"I said I had and left it at that. He asked me to come out as soon as I was free the following afternoon, and he gave rather vague instructions on how to find the house.

"When we'd rung off, I sat and thought for a long time. What shocked me more than the fact that he was drunk so early in the day was the way he sounded. There had been no trace in his voice of the forceful, alert friend I'd last seen only two years earlier. Even the divorce, by all accounts extortionate in its settlement, couldn't have affected him as badly as that. He sounded as though he were speaking from a world far away from the world I lived and worked in.

"I wasn't the least bit surprised the next morning when my answering service passed on a garbled message from Jeff Aitken, asking that I postpone my visit because something had come up and saying that he'd be in touch with me soon. But it made me more worried than ever about him and I decided to ignore the message and go out there anyway.

"As it almost always turns out when I want to get away early, I had a couple of difficult patients that afternoon, who, on the pretext of some trivial ailment, regale me with lengthy descriptions of their family or emotional problems. Other appointments got backed up, and the sun was already beginning to set as I was inching my way up the car-jammed Don Valley Parkway. By the time I was driving up Jeff Aitken's driveway, after several wrong turns, it was already dusk.

The house, viewed in the half-light, might well have been designed for a Hollywood mystery movie. A genuine Ontario Gothic, the third-floor dormer windows were graced by turrets, the lower sash windows and ground-floor veranda framed by fanciful fretwork. A vintage British Jaguar, which had not passed through a carwash for several seasons, was carelessly parked in front of the house. No light was showing in any of the windows so I walked down an overgrown pathway at one side of the house. It led around to a backyard and a kitchen door that stood ajar. Beyond that, along a passageway, I could make out a dim, flickering light.

"I knocked on the door a couple of times, but there was no reply. So I stepped inside. I don't think I'm just imagining it now, but I hated that place the moment I set foot in it. I'm not superstitious or easily scared, but, cliché though it may sound, the place felt evil. And it wasn't just because the kitchen smelled of rotten food, like a lot of cheap apartments I'd been in while I was a student. In the semidarkness I could see that the sink was piled with unwashed dishes and the overflowing garbage can was surrounded by empty bottles.

"There was the faint sound of music and talk coming along the passageway from the lighted room, so, despite my uneasiness, I walked through. The light and sound were coming from a TV set, turned down low, that was showing one of those fatuous early-evening reruns. Jeff was sitting across from it on a sofa, his head back, mouth open, snoring. On the coffee table in front of him were the remains of a meal, an overflowing ashtray, a half-empty bottle of vodka, and an empty glass.

"Jeff looked awful. He'd been handsome and well-built when I'd known him at university, a successful linebacker with the varsity team. But now he looked a mess, pale and flabby, with a paunch pushing out behind the T-shirt and jeans he was wearing. He'd lost a lot of his hair, and what was left was matted to his forehead with sweat.

"I was tempted, for just a moment, to walk out of there and leave him in peace. But I knew I couldn't. We really had been very close and, despite the time that had passed and the changes I saw in him, I was still very fond of him.

"So I reached over and shook him by the shoulder. He woke up very slowly, rubbing his face and not even noticing me at first. When he did see me, he stared at me without saying anything for more than a minute.

"'Oh ... oh, Jack,' he said eventually, "you're here. You ... you didn't get my message?'

"'I did,' I said, 'but I was worried about you.'

"He nodded. 'A lot of people seem to be,' he said. 'But look, why don't you sit down and I'll get you a drink. Only have vodka, and some beer.'

"I said I'd have a beer. Attempting to display the briskness he used to have, he cleared away the remains of the meal, emptied the ashtray, and brought me a beer. He dropped a handful of ice into his own glass and added some vodka. When I'd know him earlier, he neither drank nor smoked. He turned on a table light beside the sofa and switched off the TV before he sat down again. In the light I could see how ill and tired he really was.

"'I'm glad you came out anyway,' he said. 'This morning I panicked. I just haven't been seeing anybody lately. But I know I need to talk to somebody about all this. . . .'

"I said, 'Is it the divorce that's been the problem?'

"He said, 'Oh, that was just the start of it. It was hard to take, you know, losing touch with Sheila and the kids, and not any easier because it was mainly my fault. Hurt my pride, of course. And I don't blame Sheila for trying to squeeze as much out of me as possible. But I'd have got over that. It's what's been happening to me since that's been the real problem.'

"I waited to see if he was going to explain, but he didn't say anything more, just sat there staring in front of him.

"So I said, 'Look, Jeff, surely the real problem is that you've shut yourself away out here. You've got friends, colleagues, who respect you and wouldn't hesitate to help and support you through this trouble, if you'd only give them the chance. Surely you're not so hard up that you can't afford an apartment downtown where you could be in touch with people?'

"He agreed that that was true and said, 'I probably will do that eventually. But for the moment I feel it's best for me to work things out here by myself.'

"It was obvious that he'd have preferred me to change the subject. But there was no way I could do that.

"'Oh, for God's sake, Jeff,' I said, 'I've only been here a few minutes and it's plain to me that you aren't working anything out. Brooding up here alone — that isn't like you. Drinking and smoking — you never used to do that. You must know damn well that it's not going to solve anything.'

"I was hoping to provoke him, but all I got was a shrug. As though I'd reminded him of his need he reached for his glass and took a deep drink.

"You're a good friend, Jack,' he said eventually, 'but you don't know enough to understand why I'm here. When the divorce went through, it was convenient for me to move in here, because I'd inherited the place and it was vacant. But there's a lot more to this house than that. What you may not know is that my father killed my mother and my sister here and then committed suicide himself. I was only ten at the time, and was away in England at his old prep school. By the time I arrived back in Canada, the family had been buried. I was too young to understand what had happened. Ralph Mooney, who'd been a close friend of my father, was appointed my guardian, but he didn't tell me very much. All I've managed to find out meanwhile is that my father, who was a forensic surgeon with the city coroner's department, was made some sort of scapegoat in a malpractice suit that had political undertones. Like father like son, so now I'm accused of malpractice. I'm here trying to come to terms with him, with my father.'

"Although Jeff had never said anything about it during our time at medical school, I had later heard about the scandal surrounding his father's death. I said to him, 'I did here about that, Jeff. But I don't understand what you mean by coming to terms. Nothing is going to alter the past.'

"He stared at me and then took another drink. 'I wouldn't have thought so either,' he said very slowly, 'until I came out here. You know, I'd never been in this house until I moved here. My father bought the place just before he killed himself, and the executors of his estate leased the place to a farmer immediately after his death. Until I went to university, I lived with an uncle and aunt in Kingston. Then I got married and lived in Toronto. When things began to go sour between Sheila and me, I terminated the farmer's lease in order to move the family out here. But it was too late and Sheila refused to move. While we were separated, I did live in an apartment downtown, because I still hoped we'd get together again. When it was all over, I just knew that I had to come and live here.'

"There was a sort of resigned finality about the way he spoke that made me very uneasy. And yet, a glance around the room was enough to confirm that he'd done very little to make the place more than barely habitable. Apart from the sofa, coffee table, TV set, and a chair, there was only a divan bed in the corner with a rumpled quilt on it.

"'Well, surely you don't mean to settle out here?' I said.

"'Settle?' he said, and an odd expression crossed his face. 'No, all I've got to do here is settle with . . . with my father. I would never have believed it, but ever since I've been here I've had the sense that he's still here. I know that's weird, and it frightens the hell out of me. But I know I have to stay until I've discovered whatever it is that has to be settled between us. . . .'

"And then I suddenly realized that the expression on his face was one of suppressed terror. Before I could say anything, he went on, 'I know you're probably thinking that's morbid, purely imaginary. I've never believed in the afterlife or any of that stuff, but I do feel he's here, all the time, even right now, at this moment. And when I drive out to get food and things, I just know I have to come back here and face him.'

"I tried to interrupt him and said, 'But, Jeff, you know that's just because things have been rough for you.' But he held his hand up, shaking his head.

"'There's more to it than just having the feeling he's here,' he said. 'Whenever I lie down to sleep over there, every time, I have the same dream. Somehow I'm looking down from above at myself stretched out on that bed, and there's a man — it's my father, I'm certain — bending over and doing something to me. I know that I have to wake myself up or something terrible will happen, so I wake up; and I'm lying there alone. It seems to happen only when I lie down on that bed, so that's why the only time I get any sleep is when I sit up here. And why I need this stuff, to help.' He reached for his drink again and took a deep gulp.

"'What can I do to help, Jeff?' I asked. 'Because something has to be done.'

"After staring at me for a moment or two, he said in a more ordinary tone of voice, 'Nothing you can do, old chap. For the moment, anyway. I appreciate you coming out here, Jack, and I know you must think that this is all a lot of nonsense, but it's something I have to work out for myself. Don't know how long it's going to take. But I do know I have to face it, here, on my own.'

"Suddenly I was really angry with him. 'That's idiotic,' I said. 'You can't go on like this. You're killing yourself.'

"'No,' he said, very calmly, 'that's the last thing I have in mind. I just need time. And I'm sure that when I'm past this, I'll need your help. So don't worry. Crazy as all this sounds, I can handle it.'

"'Have you tried sleeping pills?' I asked. 'Probably what you need most is a good night's sleep.'

"'Oh, yes,' he said, 'I've tried those. They just don't work, and besides, I've never liked using them. But look, I'll tell you what, give me another week out here. If you haven't heard from me by then, call me. I'm certain I'll have myself straightened out. Okay?'

"I really wasn't convinced he would, but I agreed. And he did seem a bit steadier, more like himself, as he walked me out to the car. As I drove away I saw him in the mirror wave to me once and then turn back toward the house. For all my worry about him, I was immensely relieved to be out of that house.

"The following morning I called Ralph Mooney, told him I'd been to see Jeff, and asked if we could get together as soon as possible. He suggested that I come to his office right away.

"'Ah, Ludlow,' he said, still very much the professor. 'I'm most grateful to you for involving yourself in this matter.'

"'It's the least I can do,' I said. 'We were very close friends.'

"'Indeed, indeed. As were his father and myself in our time. That's why Claude Aitken named me as his executor and Jeff's guardian. So how is Jeff?' He looked at me anxiously.

"'Not very well,' I said. 'He's still drinking too much and neglecting himself. And you're right, it's not doing him any good being out there on his own. Especially in that house.'

"'Why do you say that?' he asked nervously.

"'Oh, because of what happened with his family there,' I said.

"'You know about that?'

"'I had heard something about it,' I said. 'And Jeff brought it up while I was with him. At the moment, he seems obsessed with memories of his father. It's very disturbing. He's even having nightmares about him, so he's getting very little sleep.'

"Mooney looked very upset by this. He stared down at his desk and said slowly, 'I've always been afraid of something like that happening. The fact is that I know more of the details of that affair than anyone else, more than even Jeff knows. He was so young when it happened that I couldn't bring myself to tell him more than I had to. And since then, whenever he's asked me about it, I've always managed to avoid telling him more. I just haven't wanted him to dwell on it.'

"He sighed heavily and sat clenching and unclenching his hands on the blotter pad in front of him.

"'So now it seems the past has caught up with him. It's a bad business. How much do you know, Ludlow?'

"'Just that Jeff's father was forced to resign because of some scandal,' I said. 'Not of his making, as I understand. And that he killed his wife, his daughter, and himself.'

"He nodded slowly, 'Given the kind of man he was, there was nothing else Claude could have done. He was a brilliant man, very correct and very sensitive about his good name. His autopsy on the victim of a politically touchy case of malpractice was suppressed and then somehow got leaked to the press. In the course of a subsequent inquiry, he was made the scapegoat and felt obliged to resign. And a couple of weeks later he took that dreadful step. And of course that made it virtually impossible for those of us who knew the facts to exonerate him publicly. It appeared to be an admission of guilt, exactly the opposite of what he intended.'

"He seemed very shaken by the recollection.

"'Did you have any inkling of what he was going to do?' I asked.

"'No,' he said, 'but I still blame myself for not sensing how deeply disturbed he was by the scandal. And he went about doing what he felt he had to do as precisely as he'd done things all his life. He and the family were living out in that farmhouse then. He got together his papers and his will, wrote me a letter, and mailed the package to me. Apparently he then drugged his wife and daughter by adding a sedative to their food and gave each a lethal injection. He'd lost his mind, of course, and as a final ghastly touch, he embalmed both of the bodies and laid them out on a bed. Then he injected himself and lay down beside them.'

"Mooney was having difficulty controlling his voice. I felt sorry for him.

"'The following day I received the papers and his letter,' he said. 'The letter was typical of Claude. He told me what he was about to do, how he would do it, and why he felt obliged to — because his good name was worth more to him than life itself and because he could not bear his family to endure any further shame. His only regret was that Jeff could not go with them, and he asked me to do whatever I could to shield Jeff from repercussions of the scandal and to act as his guardian.'

"Mooney got up slowly and walked over to the window, struggling with his feelings. I asked him if Jeff had ever been shown that letter.

"'No,' he said, 'nor have I ever told him about it. Claude asked specifically that I destroy it as soon as I had read it. Obviously he didn't want it brought up as evidence at an inquest. As it turned out, the inquest was handled very discreetly, and, for once, the press was persuaded not to sensationalize the tragedy.'

"He didn't say anything more for several minutes, then he turned back to me, working his shoulders as though he were trying to shrug off the unhappy past.

"'What I can't understand now,' he said, 'is why, after all these years, Jeff is tormenting himself about all that. And why he has chosen to go back to that house?'

"I thought about that for a moment, then I said, "Possibly it has something to do with guilt. If he does believe there's any justification to these complaints of malpractice against him, he may be feeling that he has let his father down. Maybe, that's what he means when he says he has to settle with his father.'

"Mooney looked agitated again. 'You don't think,' he said sharply, 'that Jeff has any idea of . . . of taking his life, do you?'

"'No, I don't think so,' I said. 'In fact, he went out of his way to assure me that he hadn't anything like that in mind. But as I told him, he'll kill himself with drink in the long run if he doesn't pull himself together.'

"'Well, I'm not at all happy about his being up there alone,' Mooney said. 'There's something dangerously morbid about it, particularly in light of how his father died there. Could you possibly make one more attempt to persuade him to leave that house and move back into town? Then perhaps we could arrange some psychiatric help.'

"Although I doubted that I could persuade Jeff to come until he himself had made the decision to leave, I said I'd try that evening. Mooney thanked me profusely.

"When I got back to my apartment after a long frantic day at the office, I was exhausted. I sat for a long time trying to figure out some way of persuading Jeff. The bizarre details of the way his father had killed his family had left me very shaken up. And for all my skepticism about the spirit world, I couldn't help wondering if in some inexplicable way Jeff wasn't a captive, even a belated victim, of that occurrence. Even the knowledge that Jeff didn't know fully what had happened there did not convince me that what I was thinking was nonsense. I was haunted by the sense of evil I had encountered when I stepped into that house, and by the ill-concealed terror I had detected in Jeff.

"I called Jeff's number three times during the evening. I wasn't altogether surprised to get no reply and I suppressed my uneasiness by imagining him sitting asleep before his TV set. In the end I decided to go to bed early and drive out to his house in the morning. But I just couldn't sleep. My own dreams whenever I dropped off became confused with Jeff's nightmare, and I kept seeing his pale, fearful face and hearing his shaky voice. I gave up my attempt to sleep, got up, and dressed again. It was nearly midnight.

"I got in my car, drove across town, and headed north up the parkway. I kept rehearsing in my mind various arguments that might persuade Jeff to drive back and stay with me. There was very little traffic on the parkway, even less beyond it, and I didn't pass any cars as I followed the maze of narrow, unpaved roads that led to Jeff's house. There were no lights in the few isolated farmhouses I passed, and each of them looked eerie and unreal. They looked as if they were floating on a low white mist that covered the fields, which were lit by a full moon.

"Just as I'd done before, I missed the turn to Jeff's house and had to double back. At last I made it out in the moonlight, looking more sinister than any of the houses I had passed. As I drove quietly up the driveway, I could feel fear growing inside me. The front windows were dark, but the sight of Jeff's rundown Jaguar parked in front was somewhat reassuring.

"I walked around the side of the house. Immediately the sense of dread I'd felt before closed in on me. The kitchen door was ajar, but there was no glint of light from the room along the passageway.

"You said to me earlier that you think doctors are indifferent to death because we're familiar with it. It's not true. In fact, we're more sensitive to the air of death, and I sensed it in that house at once. I stood outside for a long time, telling myself that I was just being stupid because of what Ralph Mooney had told me. It took every shred of courage I could gather to open that screen door and step inside. I was cold and an icy sweat was pouring down my face as I walked slowly, and as quietly as I could, toward the door to Jeff's room. Before I reached the open door I could make out Jeff, fully clothed, lying on the divan under the window, bathed in moonlight.

"I remember that for a moment, I felt relieved that he was lying asleep, and had perhaps overcome his nightmares. But as I reached the door, I noticed a smell that was oddly familiar. I stepped over to the table lamp and switched it on. Jeff was lying on his back, dressed in a business suit and tie, his face very pale and composed. The smell I remembered from those anatomy sessions in medical school — formalin. Even before I reached over to touch his neck I knew I would feel no pulse. Jeff was dead. And he had been embalmed.

"I don't remember anything more until I was outside again, shuddering as though I had a fever, frantically getting into the car and trying to light a cigarette.

"I don't know how long it took me to get control of myself. My immediate impulse was to start the car and drive as fast and as far from that dreadful house as possible. But my hands were shaking so violently that I couldn't turn the ignition key. Images of Jeff lying dead, and thoughts he and Mooney had told me, kept swirling through my mind. I've never felt so horrified, and I doubt if I'll ever be totally free of that feeling.

"When at last I calmed down a little, I tried to decide what to do. Maybe what I should have done was call the police, tell them what I'd found, and let events take their course. But the prospect of standing up before an inquest, of testifying that I believed that a man dead almost thirty years had killed and embalmed his son, was much more than I could face. I'd been the last person to see Jeff alive. Maybe I'd be accused of having killed Jeff in some awful fit of madness that drove me to repeat his father's repulsive crime. And eventually Jeff's children would inherit that frightful house . . . and someday . . . ?

I was lighting another cigarette when the idea came to me. You may find this hard to accept, but it was what I knew I would have to do. I've thought about it over and over again in the years since, and I still don't see what else I could have done. And yet I still find it hard to live with.

"I got out of the car. I was very calm, and I felt almost as though I were involved in a dream. Or a nightmare. I walked back into the house and into the room where Jeff was lying. There was a bottle of vodka, almost full, on the coffee table, and a pack of cigarettes and some matches. I splashed most of the vodka on and around Jeff's body and dropped it on the quilt at the edge of the bed. In less than a minute the quilt, made some sort of synthetic fibre, began to smoulder, and very soon glowing worms of fire were spreading out toward the still body. I switched off the lamp and watched until the blue flames of igniting spirit were dancing around Jeff's corpse, then I left.

"I drove to the end of the driveway with my lights off and parked by the side of the road. Before long a tongue of flame burst out a side window and caught the overhanging veranda. It raced along the dry side of the house. Soon the front windows burst out in flame and shot a storm of sparks into the air. When the roof was alight. I drove to the nearest farmhouse, roused the farmer, and used his phone to call emergency.

"Most of the roof fell in as I got back there with the farmer, and by the time the fire trucks arrived, there was very little left of the house."

Jack Ludlow, looking haggard and exhausted, sat looking down at the dinner table. Before saying anything more, he glanced at my face, trying to gauge my reaction. "There were no awkward repercussions," he said very quietly. "What I told the police was accepted without question. I told them about visiting Jeff and about his depression and drinking. And I told them about calling him several times on the night of the fire, about driving out there because I was worried, and about finding the house so engulfed in flame that I couldn't break in. What else could I have said?"

I just said, "I think you did the right thing, Jack, the only thing possible."

"You're the first person I've told this to," he said. 'Because I trust you." Then he thanked me for dinner and went home.

I've never been convinced that confession is invariably good for the soul. It may be better for some of us to keep our guilty secrets to ourselves and to learn to live with them. It haunts me now that it might have been better for Jack Ludlow never to have told me that story. Two weeks after he told me, I had a call from his lawyer, who told me that Jack was dead and that he had named me as executor of his will. Apparently, the night before, he had smashed his car through a barrier on the Don Valley Parkway and had been killed instantly. Perhaps because I sounded so shocked by the news, the lawyer added that the police believed that he had been drinking heavily before the accident.

The will was simple enough: he left most of his estate to his only close relative, a sister living in Alberta, and the remainder to medical research. But there was a recent codicil requesting that his body should not be embalmed but should just be cremated.

6

The Forerunner

We all accept that we're going to die someday, but few of us like to dwell on the fact, and I'm certain that even fewer of us would welcome the foreknowledge of how and when we are to die.

Those of us who earn a livelihood from humdrum occupations in plants or offices are rarely reminded of the reality of death unless we read about it in the papers, glimpse it on television, or suffer the loss of a friend or relative. There are occupations, however, where the possibility of death, sudden death, is an ever-present shadow.

The fishermen of Nova Scotia, like fishermen everywhere, have learned to live under such a shadow, fully aware that every time they take their boats out it may be the last time. They understandably share a more fatalistic attitude toward death than the rest of us. They also share an odd superstition, possibly brought over with them from a Scottish homeland where life was as harsh and often as brief as that which they lead along the Maritime shore; it is the superstition of the forerunner.

A forerunner is a ghostly apparition that appears as the image of a person who will shortly die and is most usually seen by the victim but on rare occasions by the victim's family or friends. Forerunners, however much they may be feared, are not a subject that many Nova Scotians care to discuss. It's felt, I suspect, that to talk about them openly might be to invite a visitation. And after all, very few of those who have been confronted by a forerunner have lived long enough to tell the tale.

I'm not a Nova Scotian, but there was a time when I used to go to the province for a couple of months every summer. I liked the freshness of the salty air and the green of the countryside and, most of all, the people there, who for all the hazards of their work knew how to savour the small pleasures of life. Putting my own work and pressures of city living behind me, I'd rent a small vacation cottage from a friend in one of those little fishing villages along the west coast of Nova Scotia. The few dozen families who live in the houses stacked around the steep sides of the cove there depend for their living on inshore fishing, following the seasonal shoals of caplin and herring, dragging for scallops, and trapping lobsters. The tides there run high, so from week to week the rhythm of work is different. Sometimes the boats are out all night, sometimes during the day. I would sit on my front porch and watch it all, occasionally sharing a conversation with one or another of the locals who had some time to spare. It was there that I listened to the story of a man who had once confronted a forerunner and had managed to survive.

Since as far as I know he's still alive, I'll call him Hamish McPhail, a name that wouldn't be out of place in Nova Scotia. I got to know him because he was the only local man with enough time on his hands to stop by for a chat three or four times a week. He is a tall, lean man with that bright red hair that is common among Celts and is allegedly matched by a fiery temper, which in Hamish's case it certainly isn't, for he is as gentle and reflective in speech as he is in his attitude toward life. He would sit beside me on the porch and talk easily about the village and its people, sympathetically but not uncritically, and always with a dry sense of humour. Inevitably his talk touched often on the business of fishing, and it struck me as odd that a man who could talk so knowledgeably seemed never to go out fishing by himself. Eventually, I felt I knew him well enough to ask him why. He pondered the question for a few moments. Then he told me that his father, a widower, had gone down with the family boat about seven years before. After that he worked with other fishermen whenever they needed a spare hand. He wasn't too hard pressed for money because he wasn't married and had inherited his parents' house out along the shore road. After his cousin had been lost in a storm the year before, he had decided not to go out with the boats anymore. Whenever he needed a bit of extra money and there was a heavy catch, he'd go down to the dock and help off-load the boats. Beyond that, there were always boats that needed scraping and painting and drags and nets that needed repairing — more than enough for him to get by.

My cottage was perched less than a hundred yards up the slope from the dock, and on days when Hamish didn't show up at my door, I'd spot him waiting for the boats to come purring around the headland. Later I'd see his red head bobbing this way and that amid the clatter and bustle on the dock. The next day he'd be sure to come striding up the track to take his ease with me and talk some more.

Toward dusk one evening when the boats had been out all day, I was sitting on the porch, watching them come in. Suddenly I was aware of footsteps below on the track and Hamish running up toward me. He stopped halfway and called to me that there'd been an accident and some men were burned. He asked me to call the doctor, who lived in the next village along the coast, and then to call an ambulance from Yarmouth, which was the nearest town with a hospital. I ran indoors, since it happened that mine was the nearest telephone. By the time I'd made the calls and stepped back outside, there was a dragger slowly heading in to the dock, Towing another dragger, which had black stains around its stern and was trailing a plume of smoke. There was already a crowd of people on the dock, so I decided to stay where I was. I watched as the leading boat drew in and saw a couple of men wrapped in blankets being helped onto the dock and laid out on a pile of crates. Within a few minutes the local doctor arrived in his car and bent over the injured men, applying dressings. Twenty minutes later, a white ambulance, with its light flashing, came whooping along the coast road and drew up at the dock. When the two stretchers had been eased in, it turned and roared back along the road to the hospital.

The people on the dock remained clustered there for a few minutes more, then began dispersing in twos and threes, heading home through the dusk. Again I heard footsteps just below and recognized Hamish's tall figure striding up the track. As he came up the steps to the porch, I noticed that his fair complexion was paler than usual and his lean face looked weary.

"They were lucky," he said quietly as he sat down. "They'll be all right. It wasn't their time, thank God."

I offered him a whiskey, but he shook his head. "No, thanks," he said. "There was a time I couldn't get enough of that. But I was taught a lesson.Now I never touch it."

We sat in silence for a few minutes, both of us staring down at the now-deserted dock.

"As you'll understand," he said, "there are always reasons enough why a man would choose not to go out in the boats. But, to tell the truth, I have a reason that's better than most." He glanced at me, then asked, "Have you ever heard of forerunners?"

I said I had heard a little.

"Well, I have a story about a forerunner," he said, "a true story, even if I'm the only one who knows the truth of it. About a year and a half ago, I was in the tavern up the road there on the other side of the dock. I'd been there all evening and I'd had a lot more drink than was good for me, though I wasn't drunk. It was the early fall, and I set off from there to walk home just before midnight. It was clear and calm, with a full moon, and still not very cold. I was taking my time along the shore road, and when I was nearly halfway home I saw a man on the road ahead of me, coming towards me. There seemed something familiar about him, but it was hard to be sure in the moonlight. He came towards me and I thought it was strange for him to be wearing a slicker and rubber boots, because nobody would be out fishing when it was low tide. He kept coming towards me, then instead of walking past, he stopped dead in front of me. I could see then that he was dripping water and his black hair was stuck to his head, shining wet, like a man who had been dragged out of the sea. The face was deadly white and was familiar to me, but I could see right through the face and the body. I knew at once that it was a forerunner, and I was paralyzed with fear. Then a low hoarse voice that seemed to be coming from a long way off said, very slowly, 'Hamish McPhail, you're time will be soon.'

"To this very day, I wish I'd said nothing. But I had the fear of God in me, and before I could stop myself I said, "You've come to the wrong man. I'm Hamish Red McPhail. The man you want is my cousin Hamish Black McPhail.' And indeed he was the very image of my cousin, called Hamish Black hereabouts because our names are the same. Then the forerunner let out a long awful moan and disappeared. I must have stood there in the road unable to move for a half-hour or more. Then, still shaking as if I had a fever, I walked home, fell down on my bed, and tried to get hold of my senses.

"It was well past dawn before I got hold of myself. I knew then that I'd have to warn my cousin what'd happened. I have to tell you that I never got along too well with Hamish Black. Though I don't like to speak ill of the dead, there's no denying that he was a mean-spirited man. The time my father was drowned and the boat lost, a hard time for me, he never once offered to lift a hand to help me. Never once did he hire me as a spare hand when he needed one. He'd sooner hire someone that wasn't kin of his. Not that he often needed a spare hand. He's the only man hereabouts who took his wife out in the boat with him. There's no denying that his wife, Moira, is as good a hand at fishing as any man in these parts, but it's not the custom for wives to go out on the boats. It goes without saying that they never had any children. Children would be too great an expense for the likes of Hamish Black.

"I knew from the way the tides were running that he and Moira would be going out early in their boat. So in the end I pulled myself together and walked over to their house. When I knocked on his door, he opened it right away. He was all dressed to go out, and Moira was standing behind him, ready to go as well. I asked him to step outside for a moment because there was something I had to tell him. He was surprised, but he stepped out and shut the door behind him. I told him as best I could about meeting the forerunner on the shore road and what I'd said to him. I was surprised how well Hamish Black took it. He said he knew his time would come in the long run. Maybe I shouldn't have said anything, but it wouldn't make much difference in the end. If a forerunner was looking for you, he was bound to catch up with you. It was just a matter of putting off the evil day. Then he sat down on his front step and said nothing more for a long time.

"Finally he looked up at me and said, 'Look, Hamish, a man can't be drowned if he isn't out on the water. And from what you tell me, it seems that I'm going to meet my end by drowning. You owe me a favour because of what you said to that forerunner. Now if you were to take my place in the boat with Moira, you could come to no harm. Your time hasn't come yet. So what do you say? I'll give you a fair share of whatever the catch brings in, if you'll work my boat for me.'

"Though I didn't like him any better, I did feel a bit sorry for him.

And besides, I still felt guilty about what I'd said to the forerunner. So I said I would do it. True to form, he made a hard bargain about my share of the catch, but I went along with it. So that very morning I went out in the boat in place of Hamish Black, along with his wife, Moira.

"There were a few raised eyebrows when I went down the dock with Moira and set off in the boat. Some of the older fishermen had never liked the idea of Moira fishing with her husband. They thought a woman in a boat was bad luck, and they always steered clear of Hamish Black's boat when they were out on the water. And I suppose some of the younger men had a laugh or two between themselves at me going off with Moira, for even though she was getting on to forty she was a good-looking woman.

"I'd always liked Moira, though like most other folk hereabouts I could never understand what she saw in my cousin. Still, there was no mistaking that she was devoted to him. Towards everyone else she was always warm and friendly, with never a bad word passing her lips. She was a great woman to work with, strong and quick, able to handle the boat as well as she could handle the gear. And never any complaint when the weather was rough or when the fishing was poor. But that fall we brought in some great catches and Hamish Black paid me my share, even if he begrudged it.

"I was surprised to hear that most of the time we were out with the boat, Hamish Black spent over there in the tavern, more often than not with his crony, Archie Duncan, a man as sour and mean as himself, who runs an engine shop in the village. Before that time, Hamish Black was always too tight with his money to spend it on drink. Still, I didn't think it was my business what he did with his time and his money.

"When the bad weather came, we laid up for a few months, because it was one of the worst winters in living memory. I was glad of the rest, because for once I wasn't short of money. I noticed that during that time my cousin stayed away from the tavern. At the back of my mind I had the idea that when the fishing started again his meanness'd get the better of his good sense, and that he'd risk going out in the boat with Moira like he had before. But no, when the weather got better in the spring, he asked me to go on working his boat as before.

"Something was different, though. Within a few weeks, I noticed he seemed to be drinking real hard, and that whenever we came in with the boat, he'd be standing waiting on the dock, usually the worse for drink, his mood as black as his name. I couldn't understand it until a friend of mine took me aside and told me that Archie Duncan was putting the word around that I'd tricked Hamish Black with the story about the forerunner so that I could go off with his wife, Moira, and that the pair of us were doing more than fishing when we were out in the boat.

"When I heard that, I was ready to quit. And in hindsight maybe I should have, for there wasn't a word of truth in it. Fond as I was of Moira, I'd never been the one to lay a hand on another man's wife, least of all my own cousin's. But then it struck me that if I was suddenly to quit working Hamish Black's boat, it'd seem like the rumour was true. So I did nothing.

"Of course, it wasn't long before I could see that word had reached Moira, too. Maybe some friend had told her what was being said, but more likely Hamish himself had accused her of carrying on with me. Whichever it was, she took it very hard. All the life seemed to go out of her. She worked as hard as ever when we were out in the boat, but she hardly had a word for me, and I just didn't have the heart to have the business out with her.

"If Hamish had accused her and she'd denied it, it was obvious he didn't believe her. Now he was the worse for drink every time we came in in the boat. We were bringing catches as good as ever, but sometimes he'd mutter about it being a very small catch for all the time we'd spent out on the water. I just ignored him.

This went on for nearly two months. I knew it was going to come to a head sometime. Then a year ago in July, we went out on an evening tide to drag for scallops. It was a fine warm evening when we set out and in only a few hours we dragged nearly a full load of scallops off the bank. I noticed some big vicious-looking clouds building up to the west, so I said to Moira that maybe we'd better go in. We were halfway around the headland when the storm broke. I've never seen the likes of it in July. The rain came down in buckets. The thunder would deafen you and the lightning would blind you. And the wind got up like a gale, with waves twenty feet high. Even with the engine going full out, we were being driven in on the shore. And then, with all the water we were shipping, the engine quit. I could see we were nearly in on the shore, so I told Moira to put her life jacket on, and I put mine on too. The next minute we hit a rock under the water. We were flung into the water, both of us. I thought it was the end, but the way the tide was running, we were driven into a little cove around the headland. As I was swimming toward the shore, I heard the boat smashing against the rocks and saw her turn over.

We crawled up on the beach and lay there, with the rain lashing down on us, until we got our strength back. Then we climbed up the headland to the coast road. We walked till we got to Hamish Black's house. It's above there on the road. There was no light on and no sign of Hamish when we went in, so I told Moira I'd go down to the tavern where he was sure to be, and I'd tell him what happened.

"When I went into the tavern, there was no sign of Hamish. But Archie Duncan was there, drinking a beer by himself. I walked over to him, dripping with water. 'Where's Hamish Black?' I said. 'His boat is lost.'

"All the colour went out of his face. He got up slowly, trembling like a man in fever.

"'Come outside here a minute,' he whispered.

"We went outside. The rain was beginning to ease off, but the wind was as strong as ever. 'Moira's all right,' I said. 'We got thrown out into the water and ended up on the shore. But the boat went in on the rocks and turned over.'

"He looked at me, shaking his head slowly from side to side, like a man that'd taken leave of his senses.

"'Where . . . where's Hamish, then?' he said in a choked voice.

"'What do you mean?'

"He couldn't speak for a minute or two. Then he said, 'Hamish . . . Hamish thought you and Moira were up to something. This evening, before you went out, he hid himself in the boat. In the locker up in the bow. So that he could spy on the pair of you . . .'

"We stood staring at each other for I don't know how long, till I heard myself saying, 'In God's name, his time was up.'

"A few of us went back out on the headland that night with ropes. We could see what was left of the boat, caught in the rocks. But the wind was still high and the waves were lashing over her. There was no way we could get close. We sat there till the light came and then the wind eased off. We got a rope on the boat and turned it over. Yes, he was in the locker all right. We got him out carried him up the headland, and laid him on the ground. Lying there in his slicker and boots, he looked the very image of the man I'd met that night on the shore road, his forerunner.

"After the funeral I never saw Moira again. She closed up the house and went to live with a sister of hers in North Sydney.

"So now maybe you'll see why I don't go out on the water. Forerunners would never make a mistake twice. Some night I'm going to be walking along that shore road and I know who I'm going to meet. I won't make it easy for them. But one way or another the end will come, and there's no avoiding it."

7

Ghost On Guard

There's a long tradition of stories about ghosts who stand guard over treasure, usually in ancient castles or on remote islands where pirates have buried their ill-gotten gains. But can you imagine a ghost guarding a bank in the hard commercial heart of modern Toronto? I've heard of one, yet strangely enough it wasn't in Toronto, where I live, that I heard the story but thousands of miles away in Dublin, where I was born and raised.

I go back to Dublin every so often out of nostalgia, and every time I return I notice that a little bit more of its charm, in the form of its elegant old buildings, has been replaced by dull graceless office blocks. However, many of the old pubs have survived, and I enjoy sitting around in them and listening to the locals talk, for exchanging blarney over a whiskey or a pint of stout is a sport Dubliners excel in and will never abandon.

A few years ago I went into one of those pubs in the middle of the afternoon to "wet my whistle," as the Irish put it. There was only one other drinker there, a middle-aged man sitting at the bar. I sat down and ordered a drink, and after a few moments he leaned toward me and said. "You'd be a Canadian, wouldn't you?"

I was surprised, because I'd always imagined that I resumed my native accent within a few days of returning to Dublin. But then, the ears of Irish drinkers are notoriously acute. "Sure," I said, "I live in Canada now, but I was born and raised here."

"I only noticed," he said "because I lived over there for a few years myself."

"Well, I live in Toronto," I said, "and have now for nearly twenty years."

"I lived there too for a while," he said. "A lovely city."

Conversation in Ireland is often desultory. We attended to our drinks in silence for a while in that perpetual twilight that reigns in the older Dublin bars.

"I was there in the fifties," he continued. "It was a bit dull, dull and straitlaced, you know, like Belfast."

"Oh, it's grown a lot," I replied, "a lot of development since then."

He nodded. "Not like here, I hope, with the money men tearing down every building with a bit of style, so they can put up their concrete blocks."

"It was like that for a while," I said. "But in the past ten years they've made an effort to preserve some of the better old buildings."

I was beginning to suspect that I was being button-holed for a drink, the not uncommon fate of tourists in Irish pubs. But he surprised me by asking. "Could I buy you another drink?"

He insisted that I have a double whiskey and, when we'd been served, asked if I'd mind if he moved to the stool beside me. "It's easier to talk," he said, "and I'd like to hear more about Toronto."

"Of course," I said.

"What I want to ask you about in particular," he said when he'd resettled himself, "is a certain building downtown. A bank."

"I live downtown," I said. "I know it pretty well."

"The place I mean is on the corner of Front and Yonge streets," he said. "A gorgeous little building. It wouldn't be out of place in Paris or Brussels."

"Oh, I know where you mean," I said. "I used to work for a magazine a block away on The Esplanade. And I had an account in that bank, while it was still a bank."

His lined, mobile face expressed genuine alarm. "You don't mean to tell me that they've torn it down?"

"No," I reassured him. "The bank moved out only a couple of months ago, to somewhere more modern and profitable. But the Toronto Historical Board has saved the building from the wreckers. There's been talk of it being converted into a museum or a restaurant or theatre."

"I'm glad to hear that," he said. "I have a strange affection for that building."

Little wonder, I thought. The building in question is a gem of neoclassical architecture, built in the 1880's, when Toronto was beginning to establish itself as a financial centre. Its two-storey facade is a perfect blend of decorative columns and pediments, framing tall windows; inside, the banking hall rises to a vaulted dome inset with a round skylight of stained glass — a temple to the city's commercial energy. It quite outclasses the overshadowing towers of glass and marble with which the banks have aggrandized themselves more recently.

"I think it's perfectly safe," I said. "Even the bankers wouldn't dare to tear it down."

My companion looked relieved. I was still trying to figure him out. He was quite well dressed and sounded well educated.

"Were you in the banking business in Toronto?" I asked.

"In a manner of speaking," he said with a slight smile. "I was teaching business methods and accounting at Ryerson Polytechnic. But I was moonlighting as a bank robber and holdup man."

I nodded slowly and calmly took a sip of my whiskey. The Irish love to try out jokes like that on strangers.

But, his expression turning serious, he said, "You may think I'm just pulling your leg, but I was involved in two attempts to rob that beautiful old bank. One of them was abortive, the other calamitous."

He studied my face for a while and then asked, "Would you have a few minutes to spare so that I could tell you the story?"

I signaled the barman to replenish our drinks.

"I was sponsored into Canada by an uncle who lived in Toronto," he began."That was in 1950, when the prospects for teachers in Ireland were very poor. I got a good job at Ryerson right away. As I said, Toronto was a dull place, and most of the Irish there were Orangemen from Ulster, a breed I had no great love for. However, I did have some Irish friends from the South, and the closest of them was Sean, whom I'd known in Dublin because we were both involved in Sinn Fein, the political arm of the IRA. We were young and patriotic, and it was exciting to be associated with a clandestine organization. Not that we did much more in those Dublin days than talk and argue. To tell you the truth, we were both glad to get away to Canada because it was beginning to bore us.

"However, as it turned out, we weren't away from it at all. Some of the friends we made in Toronto turned out to be Sinn Feiners also, and still active. They were particularly interested in Sean because he had a job with a shipping company out by the airport. Apparently word was out even then that there was going to be a confrontation in Northern Ireland, and the IRA wanted to raise money and stockpile arms in preparation. And naturally, because I was close to Sean, I couldn't help getting involved as well.

"I wasn't at all keen at first, I can tell you. I was doing well at Ryerson and had the makings of a career there. And besides, there was Doreen.

"Because I loved the look of the place, I'd opened an account at that bank on Front Street. But before long I discovered another reason for banking there, and that was Doreen. She was a teller there, a lovely, lively girl with gorgeous red hair, always ready with a smile and a joke and a pleasant word. Before long I was going to the bank two or three times a week, on some pretext or other, just to see Doreen and exchange a few words with her. And it wasn't long before she made it known that the interest was mutual. In the end I asked if she'd like to meet me after work for a drink.

"She said she would, and that same day we met at a bar in a hotel a little way up Yonge Street. It had a dubious reputation as a place you could find a hooker, but there weren't many cocktail lounges in Toronto at the time, and that one was one of the brightest, with a piano player and always lots of people. And in an innocent sort of way, Doreen liked excitement and a good time. She was from Edmonton, and her grandparents had also come from southern Ireland, from Cork I think, but they were Protestant, not Catholic like myself. Anyway, we didn't waste time talking about matters like that, although she liked me to tell her about growing up in Dublin.

"Before long, we were seeing a lot of each other after work. We'd go skating, and to the movies, and on trips out to Toronto Island. In those days couples didn't jump straight into bed after the first date, although we did a fair amount of necking, as you Canadians call it. It was soon clear to me that I was going to ask Doreen to marry me, and I didn't think she'd refuse me.

"Every so often, on Fridays, Sean would drive in from his job at the airport and join us for a few drinks at the cocktail lounge. Because he had the gift of gab, Doreen got along with him quite well. But because I was involved with her and because he seemed more and more taken up with his Sinn Fein friends, we didn't see as much of each other as we used to. However, one day when I wasn't intending to see Doreen, he phoned me at work and asked if we could meet for a drink. He suggested a tavern uptown where a lot of the Irish used to go.

"He looked more serious than usual, and when we got our drinks, he said to me, 'Kevin, things are going from bad to worse back home.'

"I said, 'That's a long way away. And I'm glad to be out of it. It's all talk.'

"He shook his head. 'There's going to be action before long,' he said, 'and we've got to play our part.'

"'What do you mean?' I asked. 'I don't want any part in all that. I like it here and I'm going to become a Canadian citizen.'

"'You're still an Irishman,' he said, 'and as long as the British are occupying the North, there's a job for us to do, finding money and guns.'

"'Well, you please yourself,' I said. 'If you want to jeopardize your future here, you go ahead and get involved. With that job of yours, you can get into running guns. But there's nothing I can or want to do. And that's final.'

"'But you have a friend that could help us,' he said very quietly, 'that could put a lot of hands on a lot of money. And she's Irish, too, isn't she?'

"I was so angry that it was all I could do not to punch him. 'You keep Doreen out of this, Sean,' I said. 'She's a great girl, and I won't have her involved.'

"He shrugged and said, 'We'll see, Kevin, we'll see.'

"I knew I wouldn't be able to control myself much longer with him so I got up and walked out of the tavern.

"A couple of days later, I was sitting in the usual cocktail lounge with Doreen after work, when who should walk in but Sean. He joined us, seeming his normal friendly self. But after a little while he began to tease Doreen about how rich she was with all that money at the bank so close at hand. I could see at once that she didn't think that was very funny. She became even more uneasy when he went on, with little pretense of humour, to say how useful all that money would be in Ireland. I tried to change the subject, but he continued, asking her if she, a good Irishwoman, didn't think any risk was worth taking to set Ireland free. She got up at once and said she wanted to leave. I went with her.

"Outside, she told me she didn't want to see Sean anymore. She didn't like his line of talk, even if it was meant to be funny. She liked her job at the bank and liked the people there. And she didn't know what was going on in Ireland and didn't want to know. I tried to convince her, not very successfully, that Sean had been joking, and we spent an uncomfortable evening together. When we parted, we didn't mention when we would meet again.

"I tried calling her at the bank the next day, but they said she was busy, so I left a message asking her to meet me that evening.

"She was late arriving at the lounge and looked very upset as she walked toward me. She sat down without even saying hello.

"'What's the matter?' I asked.

"'It's that friend of yours, Sean,' she said. 'He called me at work this morning. He said all they want is details of how to get into the bank and how to get the vault open. I told him that I wouldn't tell him anything and that he wasn't to call me again. Then he said that if I helped them, nobody would ever know. But that if I didn't help them, maybe the bank might get an anonymous letter telling them that I was sleeping with an active member of the IRA — you.'

"I could see that she was going to burst into tears. I pushed my drink toward her and she drank it in one gulp. I said, 'As I told you, I did belong to Sinn Fein, not the IRA, a long time ago. I don't belong now, and don't want to.'

"'Yes,' she said, 'but are the police going to believe that? Or that we haven't been sleeping together? Everybody at the bank knows how fond of each other we are. What are we going to do?'

I didn't have any answers. We sat for a long time, talking in circles, trying to find some way out of the trap we were in. I suppose it was then that I began to realize what a desperate situation it seemed to Doreen. She'd told me all about her childhood. She was an only child, but her parents, who were very religious, had been very strict and cold with her. She had been a model student, always getting the best grades and hoping, I suppose, for a little praise and love at home, but missing all the fun. Getting the job in the bank and moving to Toronto had opened up a whole new life for her. She was free to live her own life, people liked and admired and trusted her, and her prospects were good. And in me, of course, she saw the chance of having a home of her own and maybe, sometime, a family of her own. And now suddenly, through no fault of hers, all that seemed threatened. No wonder she felt desperate. And I've wished ever since that I'd seen how desperate she really was.

"We had a few drinks, to give us courage. In the end, I assured her that I'd see Sean as soon as possible and settle the matter once and for all. I didn't know how I was going to manage that, and, when she left me to go home, I could tell that she wasn't reassured either.

"I called Sean, but he refused to discuss the matter on the phone, and told me to meet him at the uptown tavern the following evening.

"When I got to the tavern, Sean was already there, sitting with two Irish acquaintances I'd met before, who were both fanatical Sinn Feiners. One of them said to me, 'We hear you're in some sort of trouble, Kevin.'

"'I'm not in any sort of trouble,' I said, 'apart from the trouble you people are trying to get me into. And I'm not going to go along with that.'

"He smiled and took a paper out of his pocket. He handed it to me. It was a copy of my membership record with the Sinn Fein in Dublin. He said, 'I wouldn't bother tearing that up. Lots more copies where that came from. You wouldn't want that to fall into the hands of the cops over here, would you? They'd have you out of your job and out of Canada before you knew what time it is. Then we'd be left having to deal with Doreen more directly, wouldn't we?'

"Before I could argue, the other Sinn Feiner leaned forward and said quietly, 'Look, Kevin, be reasonable. All we're asking of you is to help us get the funds we need. Once you've done your plain duty as an Irishman, that'll be the end of it. You have my word for it, once you've done this for us, we won't ever ask anything of you or your girlfriend again. That's simple enough, isn't it?'

"I tried arguing with them for a while, but without believing it would do any good. They had the upper hand. In the end, they told me they'd be in touch with me in about a week to make the final arrangements for the robbery. Then I left them and went home.

"When I met Doreen a day later, she could tell from my face that I'd failed, but she didn't seem as upset as I was. I said the only way out of it was for her to go to the manager of the bank and tell him exactly what had happened. She shook her head and said she'd thought about that, but she couldn't do it. It'd mean that I'd be put in prison and probably be deported, and she couldn't bear that. And besides, she said, the bank would never trust her again and might even fire her. Then she said she didn't want to talk about it anymore.

"We met for a short while every evening that week, just sitting across from each other over a drink. All her liveliness seemed to have drained away and she rarely said anything. A couple of times, as much to raise my own spirits as hers, I tried to convince her that the robbery might just come off, and then we could put the whole thing behind us. She just shrugged and said we'd never get away with it, she just knew in her heart we never would. On the one occasion when I had to go into the bank to draw some money, the other tellers stared at me in an unfriendly way, assuming, I suppose, that I was the cause of Doreen's obvious unhappiness.

"Eventually Sean called me and arranged another meeting. The plan for the robbery was very simple, and, as I might have guessed, I was expected to take an active part in it. Sometime earlier, Doreen had let slip to Sean that because she was so well thought of at the bank, she was entrusted with coming in early one morning a week to open the vault when the time-lock released itself. The next time she was on early duty, Sean and I were to drive up to the bank in a stolen van painted with the logo of an electrical contractor. Disguised in overalls and carrying empty tool cases and coils of cable, we were to walk up to the door of the bank at a prearranged time, and Doreen was to let us in. We were to cover our faces with stockings, tie up Doreen, and then overpower a bank messenger who also came in early and who at that time would be making coffee for the staff. When he was tied up, we were to strip the vault of small bills, pack these into our tool cases, and leave before the rest of the bank staff arrived. Sean was to drop me off downtown as soon as I got my coveralls off and then was to hide the van and money in a garage in the east end of the city.

"I was given the job of telling Doreen about the plan and what she was to do. We met the evening before it was to happen, and she didn't raise any objections or ask any questions as I went over the details. She just nodded and said she understood, and then got up, saying she was tired and wanted to go home. Her air of resignation made me more uneasy than I already was, and on the way back to her apartment I tried again to persuade her to call her manager and stop the whole affair. She just shook her head again. She didn't ask me in, but when we'd kissed good night, she said very quietly, 'Don't worry, love, everything will be all right.'

"The next morning I found it hard to convince myself that it would be all right. But at first everything did seem to be going according to plan. Sean picked me up in the van where we had arranged, and we were right on time as we drove downtown. Then we turned onto Front Street, and there, right outside the bank, were two police cars and an ambulance.

"Sean cursed and swung the van down a side street. 'She blew it,' he said, 'she tipped off the cops. The bitch!' If he hadn't been driving so fast, I'd have hit him.

"'She wouldn't,' I said, 'she wouldn't ever, I know that. There must've been an accident. The messenger even . . .'"

"Sean was in a panic. 'Get those damned coveralls off,' he said, 'quick, and get out. I've got to get this van hidden. And don't call me or try to see me today. Meet me at the tavern tomorrow. At eight.'

"I sat in a coffee shop until it was time to go to work, struggling to imagine what could have happened at the bank, worried about Doreen and knowing I dare not call her to find out. Of course, the truth never dawned on me then. I managed to struggle through the morning's lectures, then dashed out to get the early editions of the newspapers. There was no mention of the bank or an accident. The afternoon lectures were even harder to bear. At four o'clock I escaped and bought the afternoon editions. On the front page was a half-column headed BANK CLERK TAKES LIFE. I sat down on a bench, too shocked and sunken in despair to read any more. After a long time I did force myself to read the brief details.

"It was about Doreen, of course. She had arrived early at the bank and had been admitted by the bank messenger. She looked nervous and dishevelled, he said. After a brief conversation, she went to the manager's office to get the keys to the vault while the messenger went to make coffee. He heard a shot, ran to the manager's office, and found her on the floor. She apparently had shot herself in the head with a revolver taken from the manager's desk. She was dead when the police arrived.

"The branch manager of the bank said she had been an excellent worker, always alert and cheerful and very popular with staff and customers. The police announced that they had uncovered no reason for the tragic event and were continuing investigations.

"I don't remember anything more until I arrived at the apartment building on Sherbourne Street where I lived. There was a police constable in the lobby, and I walked past him in a daze and let myself into my apartment. A couple of moments later, there was a knock. It was the policeman. He asked if he could come in. I nodded and led the way into the living room. 'I take it, sir,' he said sympathetically, 'you've read the story in the paper.' I nodded again. 'If you've seen the victim lately,' he said, 'had you noticed any change in her manner?'

"'Yes,' I said, 'she'd been very depressed and upset.'

"'Would you have any idea, sir, what was upsetting her?'

"I'm not proud of the lie I told or the ease with which I was able to tell it. I said, 'We loved each other very much. And we wanted very badly to get married. But because I'm a Catholic, Doreen was certain her parents would never agree to the match. She took that very hard.' And then I genuinely broke down and wept. The policeman brought me a glass of water and I knew he believed me.

"I'm no prouder of the fact that I was able to stand up at the inquest that followed and tell the same lie convincingly. Everybody believed it and sympathized. The first time I went into the bank after Doreen's death, it was obvious that the staff felt for me. The manager made a point of inviting me into his office where he told me how sorry he was and how they all missed Doreen. I thanked him as graciously as I could, and left.

"What embittered me more than anything was that I had proposed to the Sinn Feiners an alternative scheme to the one we'd tried, one that wouldn't have implicated her so directly and that might not have driven her to take her life. My idea had been for Sean and myself to break into the bank at night through a fanlight in the glass dome of the banking hall and blast open the vault. They dismissed it as too complicated and risky, which from their point of view it probably was. But eventually I was to have cause to regret that idea.

"Needless to say, the Sinn Feiners did not share the general sympathy for my personal loss. As far as they were concerned, Sean and I were responsible for the failure of the robbery attempt. And they felt we should do penance by undertaking a series of other robberies on behalf of the cause. Under the threat that they would reveal anonymously to the police our connection with Doreen's suicide, they forced us to hold up three banks and burgle an explosive store in a quarry, a militia armory, and a sporting goods store, all of which we successfully accomplished.

"I still used the bank on Front Street and was still received with sympathy. About two years after the tragedy, I was cashing a check when the teller who was serving me made some remark about Doreen. I said that I still missed her a great deal. The girl said, "Well, so would we, if she weren't back with us again.'

"I stared at her in astonishment and she looked confused. 'Well,' she said, 'lots of the girls are certain her spirit is still here with us. Doors open and close mysteriously. We hear footsteps in the corridors upstairs, and I have heard her laugh myself. You could never mistake Doreen's laugh.'

"I said, 'I wish she were back, but I don't believe in all that stuff.'

"The teller blushed and said nothing more.

"To be truthful, I never got over the shock of Doreen's death, and I still haven't to this day. In a strange way the risk and excitement of what the Sinn Fein was forcing us to do helped to ease the pain. Because of our record of success, Sean and I began to develop a dangerous mood of self-confidence, and even to welcome every new assignment. It was dangerous because an informer inside police headquarters began to warn us that the police were getting onto us. Twice in a month we had to abandon daylight bank holdups because we were tipped off that the cops were waiting in ambush for us.

"The Sinn Feiners were beginning to get worried, so they called us to a meeting in the usual tavern uptown. They told us that holdups were getting to be too risky. But they needed funds, one last big coup, and they gave their solemn word — which I didn't value much — that if it came off, they'd let Sean and me off the hook, set us up somewhere in the U.S., and give us a big cut of the proceeds. We still weren't in much of a position to refuse. Then they brought up my idea of breaking into that lovely bank on Front Street during the night. They still didn't want to try blowing up the vault door. It was too dangerous. What they wanted us to do was break in during the early morning, lie in wait for the duty teller and the messenger, tie them up, and then just wait until the time-lock of the vault released, and bundle the money up and out the front door. There didn't seem to be any flaws in the plan, and so, much as we doubted their promises, we agreed.

"We watched the bank for a couple of weeks. We took note of which morning of the week a teller replaced the assistant manager on early duty. And then a stroke of luck: a construction crew began to erect scaffolding up the back wall, as high as the roof, to repoint the mortar in the brickwork.

"On the morning we chose, we seemed even luckier. There was a heavy mist, and, with no chance of being spotted, we were up on the dome with very little effort, complete with ropes and bags and a few tools. We easily cracked open the fanlight, anchored the rope, and let it down double inside to the floor of the banking hall. We dropped our bags down, shinnied down after them, and pulled the rope in after us.

We had an hour or so to kill before the messenger was due to arrive, so Sean said he'd go and make us a cup of coffee. I stood in the banking hall, to one side of the door, just in case the messenger came in early. I had a pistol one of the Sinn Feiners had given us, but I'd thrown away the bullets and it was unloaded.

"For all the ease we'd had in breaking in, and for all my experience in robbing banks, I was more nervous than I'd ever been before. Now that I was in there, I couldn't get Doreen out of my mind. From where I was standing I could see the teller's window where she used to stand, and I could almost see her there smiling at me. I couldn't stop thinking about what the other teller had said to me about Doreen still being there. No matter how often I told myself that it was nonsense, I still found myself listening for some sound of her.

"Sean came back with two cups of coffee. He said, 'I don't like the feel of this place. The sooner we're finished and out of here, the better.' I didn't say anything.

"At seven o'clock sharp, we heard the click of a lock being turned. The main door opened and closed, and there were footsteps. When the messenger came around the corner, I covered him with the pistol and said, 'Don't do anything foolish now. We're here to rob the vault.'

"He didn't show any surprise. He just put his hands up slowly, and he didn't say anything until we'd led him around to the manager's office and Sean was tying him to a chair. I'd begun to tell him what he was to do. 'We don't want any trouble,' I said. 'At eight o'clock, when the duty teller'll be arriving, we're going to untie you so that you can let her in . . .'

"I couldn't understand why he was smiling. Then he said, 'There won't be any teller, so you're wasting your time. The police were tipped off. They have the bank surrounded.'

"The bastards!' Sean yelled. 'Those Sinn Feiners sold us out!'

"The messenger shook his head, still smiling. 'Not so,' said the messenger. 'Your Irish pals were picked up last night. They were as surprised as you are. No, a couple of days ago we had a phone tip-off. Every detail, who you two were, who your pals were, when you'd do it, and how you'd do it. I volunteered as decoy, because I used to be a cop myself. So now, if you want to get out of here alive, you'll dump that pistol and walk over to the main door where you can be seen, with your hands up.'

"'Who the hell'd know about this to tip them off?' Sean said. 'I don't believe him.'

"The messenger said, 'It was a woman. She just said her name was Doreen. You know that name? She'd give her life to stop anyone from robbing this bank. And she did. I know. . . .'

"'That's a bloody lie,' Sean yelled. 'He's trying to con us. Gimme that gun!'

"I threw the gun across the floor, away from him. 'It's empty, Sean,' I said, 'Come on, the game's up.'

"So we walked out to where the cops could see us, with our hands up. We pleaded guilty, were given seven years in Millhaven, and served four. Then we were deported back here to Ireland."

I waved to the barman for a couple more drinks. My companion took a few sips from his stout, then he turned to me again.

"So you say that lovely little bank is maybe going to be turned into a restaurant or theatre?" he asked.

I nodded.

"That'd be fine, just fine," he said with a smile. "I think Doreen always had a longing for a bit of fun and the good life. It'd be a shame to think of her spending all eternity in a bank, the poor soul."

8

The Slaughter

I've always loved the prairies. From the first time I crossed them, on a train trip to Vancouver, I've been fascinated by those wide horizons and the vast arching sky that dwarfs the isolated farmhouses and those small railway towns with nothing more to boast of than an elevator and a water tower. It's only on the prairies that you get a true sense of the scale of Canada, that you can imagine what it must have been like for the Indians who ranged it freely for centuries in pursuit of the buffalo; or for the early explorers and hunters pushing westward, on foot or in canoes, across a continent that seemed to have no end.

For me, a city dweller all my life, the prairies held implications of freedom, solitude, innocence, and simplicity. I'd probably still harbour those romantic notions had I not encountered Andy McKee.

Andy Mckee is a legend in his own time. Although he's in his sixties, he's acknowledged in Toronto film circles as the best sound man in the business. Whenever a documentary producer had to go out on location, Andy's was the first name to come up as sound man. Because of his feeling for sound and his technical skill, Andy could have earned a small fortune working on commercials for ad agencies, but he loves to travel and prefers working on documentaries, even if they don't pay very well. And producers usually found that he gave good value for whatever he was paid. Quite apart from his skill in recording, he always seemed able to suggest somebody worth interviewing, no matter what the subject of the film was and no matter where in Canada it was being shot.

A couple of years ago I was hired as writer for a documentary film about the Dirty Thirties, and I was delighted to hear that Andy Mckee, whom I'd worked with before, was to be sound man for the film crew. In fact, Andy had gone out of his way to get the job because most of the filming was to be done in southern Saskatchewan, where he had grown up.

The group assembled at a motel on the outskirts of Moose Jaw, since we'd be shooting in that area first. Andy was already in the coffee shop when we all met for breakfast. And of course he was the only one of us who looked at home there. He was dressed, as he was always dressed whether he was in Toronto or San Diego, in a plaid work shirt worn over a white undershirt and hanging outside his baggy, well-worn jeans. This style didn't altogether mask the beer belly that added solidity to his short stocky body, and combined with his weatherbeaten muscular face and his brush-cut fair hair, it established the image of a farmer who had just driven in off the prairie for a day in town. But of course, as I knew, Andy hadn't lived in Saskatchewan since he'd left his father's farm and headed for Toronto more than forty years ago.

Needless to say, he was in his element. Before we had finished breakfast he'd reeled off the names and life stories of a dozen local people who could tell us about life there during the Depression, people his father and he had known when he was still a teen-ager. To hear him tell it, you'd imagine the years of drought and poverty had ended only yesterday, not four decades ago.

We were free that first morning while the producer and his assistant made some last-minute arrangements for interviews and shooting sessions, so Andy took me on a guided tour of Moose Jaw.

Although it wasn't Andy's hometown, he seemed to know every quirky detail of the city, which because of its name had always been the butt of jokes elsewhere in Canada. He showed me the drab remains of River Street, down by the railroad depot, once the wildest red-light district of the West, swarming with hookers and gamblers and bootleggers and crooks. He told me about the unending feud between Canadian Pacific Railway and Moose Jaw, where every other man, and most of the city council, worked on the railroad. He also told me about all the characters and eccentrics that the city seemed to breed in profusion, including the mayor, who not many years before, had decreed that pedestrians using the sidewalks should observe the same rules of the road as cars did on the pavement — the sort of oddity that has always kept Moose Jaw in the headlines of the national press.

We began shooting that afternoon. Inevitably, Andy proved his worth. The years in Toronto hadn't erased his ability to talk and think like a prairie boy, and, for the most part, our producer encouraged Andy to interview the people he was recording. I had little more to do than stand around and listen, wondering how Andy could recall so accurately and vividly events that had happened so long ago.

In less than a week we had almost all the material on the Dirty Thirties that we could manage to use in the film. To complete the filming, the producer wanted a day roaming the area with a cameraman, shooting silent footage of the surrounding prairies, the lonely farms, and the one-street towns with their self-important grain elevators. As we wouldn't be needed, Andy suggested over dinner that we take a trip the following day. "I'll take you back to my beginnings," he said, "the real country." The next morning at six he hammered on the door of my room, and after a quick breakfast we set off in a borrowed pickup truck.

It was well into the fall and there was a nip of frost in the air, as we headed south under the enormous sky, its blue chalked over by a high thin overcast. The prairie is crinkled by shallow ridges in those parts and occasionally cracked open by dried-up streams and sloughs so there are not many farms and some of those are abandoned and roofless.

For the first part of the journey Andy didn't have much to say, which was unusual for him. He looked thoughtful rather than out-of-sorts, and, since there was scarcely any traffic, he was able to scan the landscape and the farms we passed. The few small towns we passed through were sorry-looking places, little more than ghost towns, with a gas station, a coffee shop, and maybe a store. A few boasted weathered wooden churches and Legion halls. What few trees there were had mostly begun to shed their leaves. Every so often we would bump over the rusted rails of an unused branch line.

The farther south we went, the poorer and more desolate the land seemed, even though the sun had broken through the overcast. The farms were smaller, their fields hemmed in by barren ridges and small stagnant lakes, and in many of them the stubble had been burned off.

We turned eastward, with Andy remarking. "We don't want to cross over the American border. They might think we were running dope." We approached and bypassed the city of Weyburn, which looked prosperous enough, and headed southeast down a highway that ran alongside a railway line.

"Now we're coming to my home and native land," said Andy. "Take a good look at it and you'll understand why I live in Toronto. It's the kind of Canada that the fancy photographers sort of overlook. Dirt poor, the land and the people. It's been that way so long that even the Depression couldn't make it much worse."

The next couple of villages along the road seemed to confirm his estimate. Then we approached a somewhat larger town, Estevan, no less shabby but with several blocks of small houses on either side of the main street, and even a town hall.

"My father nearly got himself killed here in thirty-one. Might have been better for him if he had," Andy said quietly. "Miners' demonstration that turned into a riot. The Mounties shot down three of the miners. But nobody made too much fuss. They were only Bohunks from the Ukraine."

He turned east again and after a mile or two pointed out a line of small hills in the distance.

"The Saskatchewan Rockies," he said. "Slill piles from the coal mining. Mostly strip mining now. They rip it out with drag lines. That's how my dad earned enough to indulge in the luxury of farming around here. August to March, everybody worked in the mines so they could afford to farm the rest of the year."

A sign beside the road announced: BIENFAIT, POPLULATION 800. The two rows of rundown buildings hardly seemed to justify the name. Only a small white-painted Ukrainian church, graced by gilded onion domes, indicated any pretension to the finer things of life. As we cruised by, Andy pointed out a small café.

"If this town didn't still turn my stomach, we could stop off for a couple of Wing Wong's notorious hamburgers," Andy said, "but we'll push on."

He did draw over at the gates of a small cemetery opposite the deserted railway station, but made no move to get out.

"My granddad and my mother are buried in there," he said. "And those three miners the Mounties shot down — I imagine they're still around. They're the only people with any good reason to stay on here." Then he started the truck and drove on eastward.

About ten miles farther on, he turned down a dusty, unpaved concession road that ran across a hummocky, dried-out expanse of land that looked as though it hadn't seen a plow in decades. He stopped in front of a sagging gate, got out to throw the rotten timbers aside, and then drove on up a track that switchbacked over a series of barren ridges. Finally he stopped and cut the engine. He pointed to a couple of weather-worn posts standing in a tangle of withered brambles and weeds.

"There you are," he said. "The ancestral home. Hasn't improved much over the years."

He sat staring at the ruin without saying anything for three or four minutes. I didn't intrude. Then suddenly he shrugged and said, "But I didn't bring you all this way just to look at that. Come on, I have something else to show you."

He got out of the pickup and started trudging up the long parched slope beyond the ruins of the house. I followed him, glad of the chance to stretch my legs and enjoy the mild heat of the sun. He stopped abruptly and when I came up beside him, I saw why. We were standing on the edge of a bluff overlooking a broad river valley and facing a similar bluff on the far side. The clay cliff at our feet fell away about a hundred feet and was fluted by runoff. There was an expanse of bottom land, covered with bushes and weeds, between the cliff and the river, a curving tan serpent of slow water, low after the summer and insinuating its way through shoals of pebbles and silt.

"The Souris River," Andy said, "not one of your mighty rivers."

He sat down on the thin dry grass and dangled his legs over the edge of the bluff. I sat down beside him.

"Seems peaceful enough, eh?" he said. "Perfect place for a boy to grow up?"

I nodded. He turned his head to study my face for a moment, then added. "Well, I can tell, if you hadn't come with me, I'd never have dared come back. This is a terrible place."

He pulled up a strand of dried grass and chewed on it. "I'm going to tell you something I've never told anyone before. And likely I'll never tell anyone again."

He pulled the strand of grass out of his mouth and pointed down to the foot of the cliff. "My dad's buried down there," he said softly, "and he's not alone."

He kicked with his heel and sent a lump of clay plunging into the bushes far below.

"All this was my granddad's land," he said, gesturing toward the river and then toward the slope behind him. "He came out here from Ontario with the militia to put down the Métis rebellion. Afterwards he had the option of going back or settling on a quarter section out here. Why he didn't go back, I'll never know. 'Cause this is the worst quarter section in the poorest part of Saskatchewan. But then he was always a pig-headed bigoted Orangeman, not that long off the boat from Ireland, and this land probably looked better than what he had in the old country. Maybe he just did it for cussedness, because apparently there was a family of Métis squatting on it down there on the bottom land.

"He hated the Métis. Dirty Papists, he'd say, stinking heathens, the only good one is a dead one. And he meant it. I didn't know then how he got them off his land, but I certainly know now.

"Course, I'd never seen a Métis. They'd all been driven away north long before I was born. For all that he was a cantankerous, wicked old bastard, my granddad did have the gift of gab, and when he wasn't out of sorts, he'd tell me marvelous tales about the battle of Batoche. And if you could believe it, he was a hero. Killed more Métis every time he told the story. And I don't know how he managed it, because nearly all the buffalo had been massacred before he got out here, but, anyway, he was able to describe the buffalo hunts as though he'd taken part in them himself. He even had a buffalo skull nailed up in the house there. Said when he got here there were three cartloads of bones at the foot of this bluff, from buffaloes stampeded over the edge by the Métis for their pelts. He carted the bones into Bienfait when the railway was built and sold them to a dealer for fertilizer."

Andy stared down at the foot of the cliff with a sad look on his face, as though he was trying to imagine the carnage there.

"One strange thing when I was a kid," he went on slowly, "strange to me then, anyway, was that my granddad would never let me go down on the bottom land. He put the fear of God into me, said it was a bad place and I'd come to harm down there. And for good measure, he said he'd beat the hide off me if he ever caught me going down there. It was a long time before I dared to disobey him."

"How many were there in the family?" I asked.

"Only the three of us that I ever knew — my granddad, my dad, and myself. Like me, my dad was an only child, because his mother died young. And my mother died when I was only a year old. In childbirth, and the baby, a girl, died with her. Just as well, maybe: it was a hard place to grow up, a lonely place . . . and a bad place."

"You said your dad was a miner?" I asked.

"He had no choice. Every spring he'd try to get a crop going, wheat or barley or corn. But if it wasn't grasshoppers, it was drought or blight. Never once did he harvest enough to feed the horse and the cow through the winter. The topsoil's so thin that we could hardly grow the few vegetables we needed for ourselves. We might have managed a bit better if my granddad had allowed dad to grow something or even graze on the bottom land. It's good soil down there and it never dries out. He wouldn't hear of that and said he'd throw us off the farm if my dad tried. So it was mining in the winter and mostly working on the railway with a section gang in the summer. I never saw much of my dad. My granddad brought me up."

"Where did you go to school?" I asked.

"Most of the time, nowhere," he said with a shrug.

"There was an elementary school in Bienfait — Beanfate as they pronounce it in these parts. But my dad could only drive me in there when he was working the early shift. In the summer I'd have chores to do. My granddad taught me to read the Bible. Very strict on that, the old hypocrite.'

"No friends in the neighbourhood?" I said.

"No. The nearest neighbours were Ukrainians. And my granddad hated Bohunks almost as bad as he hated Métis.

He sat looking out at the river for a while, then kicked another lump of clay off the cliff.

"It was a lonely, empty life for me," he went on slowly, "and I had to fill it up from my own imagination. I used to come and sit at the top of this bluff for hours on end, looking down at the bottom land where I wasn't allowed to go. It seemed like a secret paradise to me, where I'd spot birds of all sorts and dragonflies and muskrats, bushes full of berries in the summer and fish jumping over there in the river. I just couldn't imagine what could be bad about it, no matter what my granddad said, but for a long time I was too afraid of him even to think of disobeying.

"By the time I was fourteen, however, I began to notice how much he was failing. He was into his seventies by then. Sometimes when he was talking to me he'd imagine he was talking to my dad, and often he was just talking to himself. He got more and more feeble and spent a lot of the day napping in his bed or in a chair on the porch. Because times were hard then, my dad was away working in Bienfait a lot of the time, so I was left more and more on my own. Then suddenly one day, for no clear reason, I knew I had to go down there, to the bottom land.

"It was a hot, still day in August, and my granddad had been asleep since after breakfast. I'd already discovered a gully a bit along the bluff there where I knew I could climb down. And that's what I did. The moment I set foot down there I knew I'd made a mistake. It wasn't that I was afraid of my granddad catching me there, because he was too feeble to walk as far as the bluff. But I knew that what he'd said was right — it was a bad place. I was terrified, and yet I couldn't turn back. I walked slowly in among the bushes toward the river. I started up a couple of birds and their squawks nearly killed me with fright. But I went on, too scared to look around me or even to reach out for one of the clusters of berries. I was alone, but all the time I had the feeling that I was being watched. By the time I got to the bank of the river, my shirt and pants were stuck to me with sweat and I was shivering like it was winter. I had to force myself to pick up a couple of stones and throw them in the water, and even the sound of that made me more frightened. It was no good. I knew I couldn't stay there, and I was crying as I walked back toward the gully. And then, when I was nearly back there, I saw him.

"He was standing at the foot of this bluff, right down there, in the shadow.

"I'd never seen a man as tall. He wore a wide-brimmed hat and a buckskin jacket with fringes and he was staring right at me with big black eyes. His arm was stretched out, pointing right at me, and there were strange terrifying sounds echoing all around me. I knew he was a ghost and I knew if I stayed there I was going to die. But somehow I managed to turn away and run for that gully. I only remember getting back up here and lying on the ground shivering for a long, long time. When I had the strength to stand up, I couldn't even bring myself to look back down there, and I was certain I would never go back down again.

"I was glad to see that my granddad was still asleep in his chair on the porch. If he'd been awake, I know he'd have noticed how upset I was. After a while I cooked a meal for us, not much, because we didn't have much, and then I woke him. He didn't say a lot, except to himself, and he hardly seemed to notice me as we were eating supper. When we'd finished and I'd cleared off the table, he told me to light the lamp for him, and he sat there reading his Bible with the magnifying glass my dad had bought him in Estevan. I knew my dad wouldn't be home because he was working a double shift, so when I'd done my chores I went to bed.

"Terrifying though that day had been for me, the night was a thousand times worse. Immediately I was lost in a nightmare. I could see myself lying down at the foot of this bluff. It was dark, and the darkness was full of bellowing animals and shouts and guns being fired. I couldn't move and I was splattered with dung and blood. All around me great hairy bodies were thudding down and I was certain that I was going to be crushed and buried. It was what my granddad had told me about so often, the buffalo run. And I was going to be killed.

"I woke up with my mouth so parched that I knew I must have been screaming out in my sleep, and my nightshirt was drenched in sweat. I got up, hardly able to stand at first, and went out to the kitchen to get a drink of water. The lamp was flickering, almost out of kerosene, and my granddad was still at the table with his head resting on the Bible. For a moment I thought he'd fallen asleep, but then I saw his eyes were wide open, staring at me. I reached out and touched his shoulder. It was cold, and his body tumbled back and fell to the floor with a thud. I'd never seen a dead man, but I knew he was dead. Somehow it didn't frighten me or sadden me; maybe I was glad. I dragged him into his room and laid him out on the bed, then I pulled on my pants and boots and pretty near ran all the way into Bienfait.

"The superintendent at the mine didn't like it much, but he fetched my dad. We drove back here to the house in the old Ford pickup my dad had at the time. We put granddad's body in the back and drove it back to Bienfait to the undertaker's. It cost my dad nearly every dollar he'd saved to get my granddad buried properly."

Andy got out a pouch and carefully rolled himself a cigarette. When he'd lit it and taken a few puffs, he went on.

"Nothing went right for us after that," he said. "We managed to get through the winter. But there was hardly any snow, and no rain in the spring and summer, for a second year. The whole country seemed to be drying up, and nothing grew. And there was the Depression on top of that. Nobody had any cash. And then, the last straw, the mines were struck. Now and then, relief trains'd come into Bienfait with surplus food and clothes from the East. And the miners there were digging coal out of what were called gopher holes in the banks of the Souris and selling it cheap to farmers. But stuck out here, my dad and I were living from hand to mouth. When that demonstration was called in Estevan, my dad didn't have the gas to drive into town. He had to walk to Bienfait and pick up a lift to the demonstration. As I said, he thought he was lucky not to be shot down or arrested by the Mounties that day. When he got back, walking all the way, I could see that he was nearly finished.

"That was the end of September of thirty-one. When my dad got up the next morning, he said to me, 'Andy, we're going to freeze this winter if we don't do something about it. We're going to have to gopher out some coal.'

"I pretended not to know what he meant, even though I'd guessed. 'How can we do that?' I said. 'We don't have a truck to get into Bienfait.'

"'I've been mining long enough here,' he said, 'to know there's a seam of coal all the way along the Souris. We'll gopher into the bluff below.'

"It was the first time I raised my voice to my dad. I yelled at him, 'You can't go down there. Granddad was right. It's a bad place!'

"My dad just laughed at me. 'You're as Irish and superstitious as your granddad,' he said. 'But he's dead now and we can put all that nonsense behind us. But then, of course, you wouldn't know how he dealt with those Métis squatters down there.'

"I didn't say anything because I didn't know what he meant.

"'Well, I'll tell you,' he said. 'When he couldn't get them to move off the bottom land, he just went down and shot them, the whole family, and buried them there. In those days nobody minded a Métis being shot. But it was on his conscience ever since. That's why the old devil'd never let us go down.'

"So I said to him, 'I've been down there. It's haunted, it's a bad place. I won't go down again, ever.'

"He just shrugged and said, 'Please yourself, boy.' Then he went and got out a pick and shovel. Before he left he asked me again if I would come and help him dig a gopher hole. I said I wouldn't, and I stood there and watched him walk up onto this bluff with the tools on his shoulder."

Andy gave a long sigh and I noticed there were tears on his cheeks. He brushed them away with his hand.

"There was nothing I could do to stop him," Andy said slowly. "Maybe I should have gone with him, but I was certain that something dreadful was going to happen that I couldn't prevent, that nobody could prevent. That was the longest day of my whole life. And when it started to get dark I knew I was going to have to go down there anyway. I walked up here. There was no sound from down below and the shadow was too deep for me to see anything. I called for my dad over and over again. But there was no reply. Strange to say, I wasn't a bit afraid while I climbed down the gully. And somehow I knew exactly what I'd find there. The bushes right below here were crushed flat. My dad's body hardly looked human, it was so crushed and broken and torn. There was no face left. And the smell . . . it was what I'd smelled in my nightmare — blood and dung and the hot bodies of animals. . . ."

Andy got to his feet, still staring down the bluff. "I just dug a hole with his pick and shovel and buried him there. As I say, I never felt afraid for a moment. Not even when I finished and noticed the tall figure of that Métis standing in the shadows. I threw the tools into the bushes, walked over to the gully, and climbed up. I didn't even stop by the house. I kept walking till I got to Estevan. I jumped a freight there and I kept going till I got to Toronto."

He turned away and began to walk back down the slope toward the pickup. When I caught up with him, he said quietly, "Maybe I should be buried down there. But the debt was settled, I guess, and at least he's not alone."

9

The Lady
With The Lamp

I always try to find an excuse to get out to the West Coast sometime in the early spring. It's a time when Ontario, and particularly Toronto, is insufferably boring. The weather can't make up its mind whether to improve or to be unspeakable one more time. There are patches of dirty snow in every corner that just won't give up the ghost and melt away. And people are irritable, full of an excruciating longing for warm sunny mornings when they can leave off their heavy overcoats and stride out on ice-free sidewalks.

Last April, after missing out for the previous two years, I did find an excuse to go to Vancouver on business. Of course, it rained incessantly during my first two days here, but it was amusing to hear my Vancouver friends imply that their rain was far preferable to the sleet and cold I must have suffered back East.

Naturally, I extended my trip a day to pay a visit to my friend Roger Castle on Vancouver Island. He's a librarian and a transplanted Torontonian, and I knew he'd get a lot of fun pointing out to me, in his ironic way, the advanced state of the daffodils and crocuses and the other extravagant features of his adopted Eden. I called to tell him when I'd be arriving and he said he'd meet me with the car.

Happily for me, the rain eased off in the late afternoon, and the setting sun was glimmering through an overcast sky as the float plane took off. It was calm and mistily romantic as we soared above the islands, but I was sorry that it was already daylight as we landed because I enjoy every one of the provincial capital's English pretensions, each of them so close to parody that they might have been conceived by Walt Disney. However, I hoped there might be time before I left the following day to savour the vulgarity of teatime at the Empress Hotel.

When I disembarked Roger was waiting for me, big and bearded, full of acerbic good cheer. He had found a gorgeous house right on the water in Oak Bay. I'd visited a couple of times before, and I noticed that, instead of driving there along the coast road, he was following the much longer inland route.

"The longest way around?" I said.

"It's the shortest way home," he answered. "Particularly on this day of the year."

"I don't understand."

"A haunting subject," he said firmly, "that we'll get into later over a glass of spirits."

As deftly as he drove, he steered the conversation around to the latest publishing gossip from Toronto, a subject he always relished. It was too misty to see much on the way, but in no time at all we drew up before the warm lights of his delightful rambling house. His wife, Elspeth, who wrote cookbooks, had a meal ready for us that deserved more attention than it got. As usual when we got together, we exchanged the latest scandals about mutual friends and enemies and laughed far too much. At midnight, Elspeth pleaded that she couldn't stand it anymore and went to bed.

Roger and I moved and settled in the armchairs in the den, which was no more than a space before an open fireplace surrounded by crammed bookshelves. He poured a couple of hefty shots of good malt whiskey, handed me one, and slumped down opposite me.

"So now," he said, "enough of this worldliness. I have a ghost story to tell you."

"I never imagined you'd be interested in anything so insubstantial, Roger," I said.

"Well, when a ghost gets you into trouble with the law, you have to take notice."

"Tell me."

"You remember meeting Rob Kelly when you were here last? Expatriate Irish poet, teaches at the university. He lives three houses down the road."

"Oh yes. The only teetotal Irish poet I've ever come across."

"Doesn't need drink. He's so intoxicated by poetry, particularly his own, and by those groupie women students of his, that he's on a perpetual bender. But anyway, exactly two years ago, and almost exactly at this time, I was sitting in this chair, contemplating something or other over a glass of Glenmorangie, when I heard a car drive up. There was a long pause, then somebody began hammering in a frenzied way on the front door. I went out and opened it, and there, looking as pale as . . . as a ghost, stood Rob Kelly. He was shaking all over. So I brought him in, sat him down, and even offered him a drink. For a moment he seemed inclined to have one, but then he just shook his head. I asked him what was the matter, and, after a great deal of blinking and gulping, he said he thought he'd killed a woman, run her down on the road. Given the excesses of Rob's imagination, it took some time to calm him down. After all, you don't *think* you've run someone down. Either you have or you haven't. Eventually I got the story out of him.

"Apparently he'd been out at the campus, holding one of his weekly poetry workshops. Which meant he'd read a lot of his own work, glanced at a few student efforts and criticized them, patted a few firm young buttocks, and brushed against a few pert bosoms. So he must have hopped into his Jaguar at about midnight and, in a state of high elation, headed for home and family. He went south to Foul Bay and east along Beach Drive, the route we avoided tonight. Just by the golf course, where the road goes into all those twists and turns, he came around a corner fast and, apparently saw a woman holding up a lamp a few yards ahead of him. He braked, couldn't stop in time, felt a bump, and the woman disappeared. When he came to a halt, he grabbed a flashlight and ran back along the road. There was no sign of a body or a lamp, and he said he'd searched the road and the shoulders for about half an hour without finding anything. So, he got back in the car and, when he was passing my house, saw a light and decided to get my advice. As if he weren't shocked enough, when he got out, it occurred to him to examine his front fender, he found a dent in it that he had never noticed before. That's why he arrived so shaken up.

"With my customary savoir faire, however, I solved his problem immediately. I simply got up, went to that bookshelf up there, and extracted *Tales of Old Victoria,* now out of print. Unlike most librarians, I do read books. So I was able to turn to a certain section of that book and give it to him to read. To save you the inconvenience, I'll tell you the story he read.

"It seems that just before the turn of the century, a printer from Halifax and his young bride took up residence in the lonely house beside the road on Foul Bay where that incident occurred. His print shop was in Victoria, and, although he was a good printer, he was by all accounts a bully and a boor, particularly when he was drunk, which was every night. The favoured victim of his brutality was his wife, but she remained devoted to him nevertheless. Knowing that he would be under the weather when he drove his horse and buggy home, she would stand out on the road with a lamp to guide him. And usually she got beaten up for her pains. On April 25, 1878, he was seen leaving town drunker and at a more reckless clip than usual. He ran his wife down on the road and killed her. The accident sobered him up sufficiently for him to hang himself in his barn. Since then, on anniversaries of the tragedy, various travelers have reported encountering the ghost of that young woman with her lamp on that stretch of road. Rob Kelly must have been the first to actually run her down."

"And did reading about that convince him that he hadn't killed anyone?" I asked.

"Well, it calmed him down considerably. And soon it began to appeal to the romantic side of him. The Irish rather go for that sort of thing. He still wasn't convinced that a ghost could dent his fender. But as I pointed out to him, when he's inflamed by adulation and lust, as he was that night, he could drive through a house and not notice.

Possibly he had hit something while he was parking."

"But how does trouble with the law come into it?"

"Ah, that's the next installment. I'll just fortify you for what's to come."

He refilled our glasses generously with malt.

"But were you convinced he'd seen this famous ghost?" I asked as he sat down again.

"He didn't answer immediately, then finally he said, "Not then, I wasn't. I'd always believed that ghosts were self-perpetuating. It only needed one person to say he'd seen one and forever afterward other people would imagine they'd seen the same ghost. Y'know — imagining it simply because they needed to. It was my theory then that Rob Kelly must have read or heard the story sometime before and just forgotten it. Something half-recalled — the date, for instance — might have summoned the illusion out of his subconscious. I tried that theory on him and he just shook his head. Later, when I tried teasing him about his ghost, he didn't take it very well. He seemed to brood about it. Then last April he called me up one day and reminded me that in a week it would be the twenty-fifth again. He said he wanted me to join him in an experiment. We'd go down to the Empress and have a good dinner together. Then we'd drive back along the coast road at midnight. If we both saw the ghost, I'd pay for the dinner. If only he saw it, or if neither of us saw it, he'd pay. And of course I agreed like a shot.

"We had a very good dinner. Since I was convinced I wasn't going to pay for it, I insisted on the very best, a fine bottle of wine for myself, cognac, the works. He didn't drink, of course, and although he tried not to show it, I could see he was nervous. We got in his Jaguar at about twenty to twelve and cruised out along the road. Then I think he noticed that we were a little behind schedule and speeded up a bit. As we approached the crucial winding stretch of road, I thought he was going a little faster than was wise. But I didn't say anything. I was feeling so relaxed and confident that nothing was going to happen that I almost missed it when it did happen. He swerved suddenly and I just glimpsed a light and a vague figure in white and felt a slight thud. Rob kept on driving without even glancing around. I didn't either. I couldn't have, and I was speechless. Neither of us spoke even when he drew up in front of this house. As we both got out, he picked up a flashlight. He walked forward and shone it along the front fender. Sure enough, there was a slight new dent near the end on his side. We just stood and stared at it for a long time.

"I'd been so certain I'd win the wager that I'd insisted that he pay for the dinner with his charge card. I took out my wallet and handed him the full amount. He put it in his pocket slowly, like a man in a trance. I asked if he wanted to come in for a while. He shook his head and murmured that he felt very tired and that we could talk about it all tomorrow. Then he got into the car and drove to his house."

Roger paused, stretched, and gave a deep sigh. I suddenly noticed that he looked rather tired.

"I sat here a long time and drank a lot of this stuff before I felt I could sleep. I just didn't know what to think about what I'd witnessed. It defied everything I'd come to believe. What I'd glimpsed on the road kept flashing through my mind, over and over again. Then I fell asleep in this chair.

"When I woke up, it was light and Elspeth was bending over me. A policeman was standing out in the hall, with his cap off, staring in at me and, no doubt, at the glass and half-empty bottle beside me. I got up, feeling terrible and probably looking worse, and walked out to him as steadily as I could.

"'Can I help you?' I said.

"'Well, maybe you can, sir,' he said. 'We're making enquiries into an accident.'

"I think I just stared at him, wondering if I was still asleep and having a nightmare.

"'Were you in the company of a Mr. Robin Kelly during yesterday evening, sir?' he asked.

"'Yes,' I said, 'we drove in to the Empress Hotel at about nine, had dinner there, and drove back here.'

"'Were you in charge of the vehicle?' he asked then. I told him that Rob had driven us down there and back, and I was careful to add that Rob doesn't drink.

"'Was there any unusual incident on the way back?' he asked, and he was watching me closely. My instinct was to say no, but I knew I couldn't. Elspeth was standing in the doorway, looking pale and watching me as intently as the cop. I was suddenly feeling very embarrassed. Somehow I managed to say, 'Yes . . . we saw a ghost . . . a mile back along the road . . . you know, there's a story about it. . . .'

"'I've heard that story, sir,' the cop said, and then he asked me if I'd seen anyone else or any other vehicle on the road last night. I said I hadn't. So he asked me if I'd be willing to come with him to police headquarters to make a statement. There had been an accident last night, but as far as he knew no charge had been laid.

"He allowed me time to go upstairs to wash my face and tidy up a bit, but I still looked awful. Elspeth, of course, had heard all about this ghost business between Rob and myself and thought it a lot of nonsense.
But she hadn't heard what had happened on the way home, because we hadn't spoken since. She was standing in the hallway, looking bewildered and frightened. So I took her aside for a moment and told her that it was all a misunderstanding and there was really no problem. But I told her to call Fred Dennison, our lawyer, and tell him what was going on.

"There was a police car outside, with another cop at the wheel and with Rob sitting in the back. He didn't look any better than I did. We just said hello and didn't speak to each other again on the drive into town. I noticed that there were two cops standing beside Rob's Jaguar up the road, and when we passed the place where we'd seen the ghost, I saw more cops measuring the road. I was baffled. Were they going to charge Rob with running down a ghost?

"It was all business when we got down to police headquarters. There was a young woman sitting in the reception area with a woman cop. She'd obviously been crying, and she stared at us both as we passed through. There were a couple of plainclothesmen waiting for us, and they took us into separate interrogation rooms. Mine was a cool customer, very thorough and polite and skeptical. Obviously not someone inclined to believe in ghosts. In no time at all, taking notes as he went, he had the whole story out of me, from Rob's original encounter a year before, through my incredulity, our experiment the night before, and what we'd seen on the way home. Finally he said, 'And you honestly believe, sir, that Mr. Kelly did see that apparition a year ago and that you both saw the same apparition last night?'

"'Yes,' I said, 'yes, I do.' He fetched me a cup of coffee and told me to wait while he typed up the statement. I suppose I should have asked him then what was behind all this fuss. But I was so stunned by the pace of events and so hung over that it just didn't occur to me to ask. It still seemed like part of a nightmare.

"Eventually, the detective and his colleague came back. I read through the statement. It was very accurate, so I signed it and they witnessed it, and then they went away again. After another long wait, my detective came back and asked me to come with him. He showed me into a larger room, a conference room. Rob was sitting at the table, looking pale and anxious, and so was Fred Dennison, who happened to be Rob's lawyer as well as mine. And then there was a heavyset man, bald, with a long ruddy face. A pile of documents, with my statement on top, was on the table in front of him. He introduced himself as Inspector Smyllie, a misnomer if ever there was one.

"The inspector cleared his throat in the traditional way, placed a hand on the documents, and said uncertainly. "This case is the strangest I've ever encountered in all my years in the force. At approximately 11:52 P.M. last night, Miss Ann Dowson and Miss Deborah Fleet, both nurses, were driving home from duty at the Royal Jubilee along Beach Drive. Just west of the golf club gates they came around a corner and claim they saw a woman holding some kind of light in the middle of the highway. Miss Dowson, who was driving, claims that she attempted to avoid the pedestrian, but was unable to avoid striking her. She halted her vehicle on the soft shoulder and walked back along the highway with a flashlight to locate the victim of the accident. She found no trace of the victim, but while she was searching, another vehicle came around a bend in the road, attempted to avoid her but struck her a glancing blow. Miss Dowson suffered a broken leg and abrasions. She was very lucky to survive. The vehicle that struck her did not stop at the scene of the accident, but was identified this morning by Miss Fleet as belonging to you, Mr. Kelly. Subsequent investigations confirm that fibres found on the front fender of your car, a Jaguar, match those taken from Miss Dowson's slacks.'

"I heard a gasp from Rob and suddenly he slumped forward with his face in his hands. Fred Dennison leaned over and put an arm around his shoulders. The inspector looked disconcerted for a moment, but then went on, 'In your statement this morning, Mr. Kelly, and yours, Mr. Castle, you seem to confirm that Mr. Kelly was involved in a very similar incident exactly a year ago, when Mr. Kelly believed he had struck a woman pedestrian at exactly the same location and had failed to discover a victim of the accident. Your statements also confirm that you both set out with the intent last night to prove or disprove that the victim was in fact an apparition, the ghost of a woman who had been murdered at this place one hundred years ago.'

"The inspector threw a glance at Rob and myself, gulped as though he were trying to swallow something unpleasant, and then went on, 'Unfortunately, the law does not make provision for the existence of ghosts, although I have heard this story. However, both Miss Dowson and Miss Fleet acknowledge that Miss Fleet had put herself in a dangerous position and that Mr. Kelly had little hope of avoiding her when he came around the bend in the road. Of course, we could lay the charge that Mr. Kelly left the scene of an accident, but taking into account the evidence here, I think all parties are convinced that some kind of apparition was involved. Miss Dowson's injuries are covered by insurance and she does not wish to press charges. It's my personal view, considering the way the press sensationalize everything these days, that we should play down these incidents and let them drop.'

"I could see Dennison nodding his agreement immediately, Rob waved a hand in agreement, and I, although I had a hard job not laughing out loud at the oddity of the whole affair, said that it seemed fair. The inspector looked relieved and shook hands all around, and we walked out free as birds. Now, how about a last nightcap?"

Not waiting for a reply, Roger splashed some more malt whiskey into our glasses.

"And what was Rob's reaction to all that?" I asked.

Roger just shrugged. "Well," he said slowly, "I'm not too sure. I heard that he paid lavish attention to Ann Dowson while she was in the hospital, because she's a very pretty woman. Lots of flowers and many visits. I don't know if it went further than that, because I was told about it by Janice, Rob's wife, who was rather put out by it, although she should be used to his tomcatting by now. He's been notably standoffish toward me. Probably afraid I'd tease him about the whole thing. And you must admit it is ludicrous as a ghost story. In the last few months he's been looking very morose. I hear things haven't been going too well down at the university. And I think he may have applied for a sabbatical. Anyway, now you can understand why I brought you the long way home tonight. The lady with the lamp was probably disappointed."

We resumed talk about mutual friends and recent gossip for a while and then went to bed.

I woke up with a start. Roger was shaking me. He looked very strange.

"Sorry for this," he babbled. "Had to tell you. Rob... Rob Kelly... the fool. Drove back along the golf course road last night... swerved off the road there... turned over and killed himself!"

He sat down on the bed beside me, his head in his hands. "God-damn poets... Irishmen," he murmured, "so stubborn. Can never leave well enough alone. But he always was a ladies' man."

10

The Curse of La Corriveau

Ghosts and the auto business somehow don't seem to go together. Nor was it easy to imagine a car salesman like Romeo Dionne connected with anything that was not of this world. French in name only, Romeo spoke only English and didn't seem the slightest bit interested in French Canada. In fact, he'd never been to Quebec or to the township his family came from, St. Valier, on the south bank of the St. Lawrence opposite Quebec City. Nevertheless, he was able to tell me the long and horrifying story of La Corriveau, the witch of St. Valier, as though he'd witnessed it personally, even though it all happened two hundred years ago.

I got to know him because we both drank in the same bar, The Madison, in midtown Toronto. I used to drop in there in the evenings because it was just around the corner from the magazine where I worked. Romeo was always there, priming himself for his evening job, which was selling cars in an uptown lot. You couldn't help but notice him, because he dressed the part of a car salesman, with flashy, pastel three-piece suits and gold chains everywhere, on his wrist, on the insteps of his shiny shoes, and around his neck. His face, under dark, teased-out hair, seemed to go with his seductive name: tanned, a shade fleshy, with full lips under a dark moustache, and brown eyes that were rarely still, particularly if there were any women in the bar.

At first we were merely nodding acquaintances, but one evening when the bar was quiet and I was glancing through a manuscript that needed a lot of editing in a hurry, he carried his drink across and sat at the table next to mine.

"Hello there," he said. "You're a writer, aren't you?"

I admitted I was. Within a few minutes, in an apparently casual conversation, I realized he'd learned a lot about me, while trading it for little information about himself. And I sensed that those sharp lively eyes of his, used to sizing up potential car buyers, told him even more about me than I had willingly revealed.

"Y'know, I envy you," he went on, taking a sip from his drink.

"Always fancied I'd like to write a book. About my granddad, an amazing old guy. Came from Quebec, and brought me up. It's sort of a ghost story. But I know I'm never going to get around to writing it. I'm too impatient, have too many irons in the fire. Maybe you'd like to hear it sometime?"

"I would," I said, "especially if it's about ghosts."

"Well, if you're in here tomorrow, I'll tell it to you. That's a promise. Now I have to run. Business is business, y'know. Take care . . ."

With a wave he was off, giving the waitress a ten-dollar bill and a hug as he headed out.

When I arrived the next evening he was in The Madison as usual and he waved me over to his table. Without needing to ask, he ordered what I always drank, a double Jameson. He seemed quieter than usual, even a little shy. Obviously he was excited by the idea of telling me his story, and for a change his eyes didn't range around the bar, studying the other people there. Nor did he waste any time on preliminaries.

"I come from a strange family," he said softly. "Restless, y'know. It's in the blood. Started with my granddad, I guess. He was an orphan, brought up by an aunt and uncle in a little place called St. Valier on the St. Lawrence, outside Lévis. He must have been quite a handful as a boy, because when he was nearly eighty, and raising me, he was still a character. Had a lovely kid living with him, Jenny, and she wasn't even thirty. He'd been a showman with Barnum's Circus when he was only seventeen, and I'll tell you a lot more about that later. Then he took off for Dawson City and Australia and the Congo, panning gold. After that it was Turkey, Mexico, you name it. The lot. My dad wasn't much different, only he got into the booze. With my granddad on the move all the time, he was brought up by relatives in Shawinigan, and, like father like son, he got into show business as well, on the carny circuit. Met my mother on the road, but she took off when I was only a year old. That broke my dad up. He'd been a shill, but he was really more of a con artist. When he started drinking, he got careless, was caught, and did time. That's when I got dumped on my granddad, who was running a scrap-metal business outside Hamilton. I'd probably have gone into show business too, if it amounted to anything these days. But anyway," he paused to sip reflectively at his drink for a moment, "selling cars is the same sort of racket as show business, and there's more money in it.

"I suppose you're wondering what all this has to do with a ghost. Well, it's a long story, and it began more than three hundred years ago. I'll tell it to you the same as my granddad told it to me. I was about sixteen at the time, but I remember it as clearly as if he were sitting where you are now, telling it to me. And he first heard it when he was sixteen."

That grandfather must have been a remarkably impressive old man. As soon as Romeo launched into the story, his whole manner seemed to change and his voice took on the rhythm and tone of a born storyteller. At times his tongue couldn't quite cope with the pronunciation of the French names, but he always made a good try. The atmosphere of the downtown bar seemed to fade away and I felt as though I had gone back in time and was listening to the original tale as it had been told maybe a hundred years ago.

"Two hundred years ago," Romeo began, "St. Valier was a small, dreary hamlet within the domain of the Chevalier de Lévis, on the south bank of the St. Lawrence opposite Quebec City, which was then the capital of New France. Sieur Corriveau de St. Valier, a minor nobleman, had been granted land within the domain as a reward for previous military service to France. He lived alone, apart from a decrepit manservant, in a dank stone house close to the river; a middle-aged recluse, cantankerous because the land he was granted was too small to yield the income he felt he deserved. The habitants who paid him dues for the right to farm allotments of his land disliked him intensely, and they predicted he would die as he had lived, a bitter, lonely old skinflint without an heir.

"But in the late spring of 1671, word reached Sieur Corriveau that the last shipload of the *filles du roi*, the King's Girls, had arrived at the Convent des Ursulines in the capital. These young women were French orphans whose passage from the home country was sponsored by the French court in hope of bolstering the declining population of New France, where there were few marriageable women among the settlers. Match-making, under the supervision of the Ursuline nuns, was conducted with great seemliness. Receptions were held in the convent, at which carefully selected suitors could propose marriage to the young women, who were free to accept or reject the proposals. If they accepted, they were provided by the authorities with a dowry of an ox, a cow, two chickens, two barrels of salt meat, two pigs, and the sum of eleven crowns.

"Sieur Corriveau, probably attracted more by the prospect of the dowry than a bride, dressed himself in his only good suit and hastened across the river. But he arrived late at the reception and by then almost all the comely girls had been spoken for. Of those remaining, only one stood out — a strikingly beautiful girl of sixteen, whose dark piercing gaze and haughty manner seemed to deter suitors. It was also possible that the earlier suitors were afraid of the girl because of a rumour that had arrived with the *filles du roi*. It was said that this girl, Marie Exili, was the orphan of a notorious Italian alchemist, who had been condemned for his involvement in a poison plot within the French court and had been torn to pieces by a Paris mob before he could be executed. It seems unlikely that Corriveau knew of this at the time or that he ever found out, because he asked to be introduced to the girl and proposed marriage. After staring for a long moment at the dowdy, middle-aged man before her, Marie Exili disdainfully agreed to accept him. A wedding was arranged at the church in Lévis a week later, and in due course the dowry of livestock, provisions, and money was delivered to the manor of St. Valier.

"Although Sieur Corriveau and his bride were more than twenty years apart in age, that was the least of the differences between them. She remained haughty and remote, performing her duties as a wife grudgingly, and the household by the river continued to be a gloomy, neglected place avoided by the habitants. Twenty years later, in 1691, to the amazement of everyone in St. Valier, it was noticed that Marie Corriveau was pregnant, and eventually she did present her aging husband with an heir; not a son, as he may have hoped, but a daughter, christened Marie Josephte Corriveau.

"The child brought little apparent joy to the family. Raised almost entirely by a nursemaid, she was rarely seen beyond the overgrown garden of her home. As she grew, however, it was observed that she had inherited her mother's dark good looks. When she was fourteen, her father, who was in his seventies and who had been ailing for some time, fell into a coma and died within a few days. Since he had no relatives in New France and no friends, no effort was made to discover whether his death was due to natural or unnatural causes. Inevitably, however, there were rumours that his wife had used the fatal skills learned from her father to help nature take its toll.

"The habitants of St. Valier were a superstitious lot, and, reinforced by their dislike and fear of Marie Corriveau, it was not long before the belief was established that not only was she a murderess but that she practiced the black arts as well. Word went around that on nights of the full moon she could be seen crossing the river with her daughter to the Ile d'Orléans, which was also known as the Isle of Sorcerers and reputed to be the gathering place of a coven of witches.

"It did not take long before news of Marie Corriveau's esoteric skills reached the drawing rooms of the capital, across the river. Eventually one of the more curious and daring grandes dames ventured a visit to the gloomy mansion of St. Valier and was thrilled to discover that its mistress was willing to tell fortunes. She wasted no time in letting her friends know of the service, and soon no woman of fashion would dare confess that she had not paid a visit to St. Valier, despite the fact that the fee for a consultation was very high.

"Witch though she may have been, Marie Corriveau was unable to defy the passing of time. By 1735, already in her eightieth year, she was a withered, bent crone who spent much of her time confined to bed, too ill to receive visitors. Her daughter, however, unmarried and already middle-aged, had inherited not only her mother's haughty good looks but her skills in divination, and often she substituted for her mother in telling fortunes.

"Late in the fall of 1740, the two vicious watchdogs that were allowed to roam the grounds of the mansion after dusk began to howl at midnight and continued to rend the darkness until dawn. Neighbours guessed that the sinister old woman had finally reached her end. They were right, and a couple of days later, attended only by her daughter and with a minimum of ceremony, she was buried in the churchyard of Lévis.

"To distinguish her from her mother, with whom she shared the name of Marie, the spinster daughter was referred to locally as La Corriveau, a name that would be mentioned with a peculiar dread along the St. Lawrence for many generations.

"La Corriveau's reputation as a fortune-teller soon exceeded that of her mother. In addition, she let it be known to her rich clients that she was skilled in preparing love philtres and other potions that would cure minor illnesses of body and mind. This increased the traffic from the capital to the mansion in St. Valier, attracting ladies from the very highest levels of Quebec society, and adding considerably to the fortune that La Corriveau had inherited from her notorious mother.

"At about this time she also began to receive calls from a quite different kind of visitor. Louis Dodier was the most enterprising and prosperous of the habitants who paid dues to the mistress of St. Valier. He was a forceful, handsome man in his early forties, a widower with four grown sons, who worked as hard during the day as he drank during the evenings in the Lévis taverns. Those who knew him well were not surprised when it became obvious that he was paying court to La Corriveau. Although she was already sixty-six, she had retained much of the inherited dark beauty that had faded more rapidly in her mother. But what was more important, as Dodier's acquaintances quickly recognized, was that the spinster was a very rich woman with no known heirs. La Corriveau's evil reputation was no deterrent to Dodier when set against the prospect of enjoying a comfortable and prosperous old age as the Sieur of St. Valier.

"Dodier was under no illusion that it would be easy to win La Corriveau's favour. His first approach was on the pretext of offering to repair her mansion, which, after decades of neglect, looked in danger of collapse. His offer, if coldly received, was eventually accepted and, for a miserly fee, he was told to undertake only the most urgent repairs. He took his time with the work, pleading the demands of his own farm, shortages of material, or bad weather to delay progress. But he took good care to visit the house several times a week and to invent excuses to consult La Corriveau about the work, hoping to ingratiate himself with her and learn more about her habits and disposition. After more than a year, he seemed to be no nearer his real object than when he had begun. La Corriveau remained aloof, despite his boasts to his drinking cronies in Lévis, and he was unable to delay repair of the house much longer. But much larger events came unexpectedly to his aid.

"Early in the spring of 1758, news reached Quebec City that in Acadia the great French fort of Louisbourg had fallen to an English invasion fleet and that another English force had begun to advance on the capital from the south. There was no great alarm among the authorities within the walled city, who were convinced that the fortress towering above the St. Lawrence could withstand any English attack. Among the unprotected habitants on the south bank, how-

•ver, there was a growing panic. The Chevalier de Lévis and his force of local militiamen had already been assigned, in the event of an attack, to cross the river and defend the downstream flank of the city. The remaining inhabitants would be left defenseless on the south bank, exposed to the ill-disciplined and rapacious English troops, who would certainly set up siege batteries there.

"Dodier lost little time in bringing this alarming news to the woman he was determined to marry. He pointed out that the old house by the river would certainly be in the forefront of any siege. He added that two of his sons had cleared some land and established a farm too far inland to be threatened by any hostilities around the capital. Then, in as impulsive a manner as he could manage, he proposed marriage to La Corriveau, assuring her that although their stations in life were very different, their dealings had left him full of admiration and respect for her.

"La Corriveau, despite the sheltered life she had led, was no fool. She had long ago realized what lay behind Dodier's interest in her but, on the other hand, he was the only ally available in the face of such danger. Whatever faith she may have had in her esoteric powers, she was certain that they would protect neither her property nor her person from the chaotic brutalities of war. She admitted to Dodier that because she was an old woman much maligned by the envy and suspicion of her neighbours, she would be defenseless if the English invaded. She said she was touched by Dodier's concern for her well-being, and so, although their marriage could only be one of convenience, she would accept his proposal. They were married, as quietly as possible, a few weeks later in the church at Lévis where her mother had long ago made a similar marriage of convenience with Sieur Corriveau.

"In fact, the English invasion fleet did not approach the capital of New France for another year. In the meantime, the daily life of La Corriveau and her new husband altered very little, apart from the fact that he moved a few of his belongings into the mansion by the river. He continued to make repairs around the building, and one of his younger sons tended to the garden. Because his wife had made it plain that she preferred him absent when she received her clients from across the river, he spent more time in the Lévis taverns. Knowing that time was on his side, he made no attempt to assert the normal rights of a husband; for he knew that if he was patient, everything would eventually be his.

"Shortly after the spring break-up, word arrived that the English fleet was only a day's sail downstream from the Ile d'Orleans. Dodier had planned for the moment. Two carts and a carriage were loaded with the most valuable of La Corriveau's possessions, and they set off at once for the farm where they were to take refuge. With a sense of satisfaction, Dodier loaded onto the carriage a locked iron-bound chest, heavy enough to suggest it contained a considerable number of coins. The journey wasn't easy over the thawing unpaved tracks, but

they arrived safely and settled in. Shortly afterward they learned tha
the English had taken possession of the south bank of the river oppo
site the capital and were establishing siege batteries near Lévis.

"The siege lasted the entire summer. Confined in a small primitive
farmhouse, with little privacy and less comfort, La Corriveau hated
every moment of her exile. When she was not sulking, she was comp
laining to Dodier, blaming him for every discomfort. And Dodier
himself, cut off from his drinking cronies, was just as morose and
bitter. Her nagging, combined with the idleness, the heat, and the
blackflies, brought him several times to the edge of violence.

"At last, however, at the end of September, the news reached them
that the English had taken the capital. Although they were warned
that the area close to the river was still plagued by bands of skir-
mishers and Indians, La Corriveau insisted that they return to St.
Valier without delay. To provide some protection, two of Dodier's
sons went with them and twice had to drive off marauders with their
hunting weapons.

"When they arrived at St. Valier, they discovered that the house
had been broken into and looted, and although it had obviously been
used to quarter troops, while filthy, it was not badly damaged. Their
return home, however, did not repair the rift that had developed
between the couple during their inland exile. One of La Corriveau's
former servants who had survived the battle was rehired and did
most of the work of restoring the house to habitable condition.
Dodier, lazier than ever, shirked as much of the restoration work as
possible and spent most of his time drinking with his surviving
cronies in Lévis.

"La Corriveau, an old woman now but still alert, spent her time
brooding in bed. Quite apart from her hatred for her husband, she
was embittered by the fact that the war had ruined her trade as a
fortune-teller. Many of the society ladies who had been her clients
had fled to Montreal in the face of the English invasion, and those
who had remained in the capital considered a visit across the river far
too perilous in times such as these. It was observed by curious
neighbours that on nights of a full moon, the old woman would
hobble down to the riverbank and stand gazing for hours across the
river toward the Ile d'Orléans. The superstitious swore that on such
nights they could detect the glow of a fire above the treetops of the
island, an indication that the reputed coven of witches still assembled
there. The more skeptical dismissed the glow as an illusion or attri-
buted it to the campfires of the English soldiers still garrisoned on the
island.

"The winter following the capture of Quebec City was a harsh one
and food was in short supply. Dodier, on the basis of his wife's reputed wealth rather than his own dwindling resources, began to specu-
late as a broker of provisions for the English garrison. A poor
businessman, his habitual drunkenness did nothing to improve his
chances of success, but his assurances that he would soon inherit the

wealth of La Corriveau, who was now well into her seventies, seemed to satisfy his creditors for the time being.

"In the spring of 1760 word reached the area that a French force, led by the Chevalier de Lévis, was advancing down the St. Lawrence in an attempt to retake the capital. Dodier, because of his dealings with the English, was anxious to return to the refuge of his son's farm, but La Corriveau refused to leave her home again, and Dodier was obliged to stay because he was afraid of losing her hoarded money. The battle that followed took place once more on the Plains of Abraham, and although the English suffered heavy casualties, they repulsed the attack on the city and forced the French to retreat. There was no military activity on the south bank of the river near St. Valier.

"Peace and order were soon restored to the region by the English military governor, General James Murray, whose fairness and honesty greatly impressed a local population long accustomed to corruption in the government. Dodier continued his speculation in food supplies, with no greater success, and by the end of the year the farmers he had been dealing with were pressing him hard for payments. More and more morose, he became more and more inclined to drown his troubles in the taverns of Lévis. La Corriveau's servant reported to neighbours many violent arguments between the pair whenever Dodier staggered home to the house in St. Valier. But, despite Dodier's bravado when he was with his friends, and despite the way he scoffed at their mention of his wife's evil powers, he never went too far with his abuse, nor did he attempt to take her money away from her. He was obviously secretly cowed by her reputation and feared the results if he resorted to physical force.

"Eventually, when his affairs seemed at their lowest ebb, Dodier was offered a solution to his problems. His four sons, still loyal to him, offered to pool their resources and become his business partners. One was a sucessful merchant in Quebec City, and the three others each owned thriving farms on the south bank of the river. It was rumoured locally, although it was never known for certain, that as part of the arrangement the sons insisted that they share equally in their stepmother's estate when she died. Nevertheless, once Dodier's outstanding debts had been settled, the joint venture seemed to prosper for the first two years; and although they remained enemies, Dodier and La Corriveau seemed to have arrived at some sort of uneasy truce within the mouldering old mansion by the river.

"Unfortunately, Louis Dodier did not take to success any better than to failure. Just when the enterprise had restored him to his former prosperity, he began not only to drink heavily again but to gamble, often with the officers of the English garrison. Drink and gambling proved as disastrous a combination as had drink and business, and it was not long before Dodier was surreptitiously drawing capital from the business to settle his card debts.

"When they realized what was happening, the four sons were outraged. Early in 1763 they confronted their father and announced that they intended to end their business partnership with him. They insisted that he repay them the amount he had squandered, and when he protested that he was penniless, they demanded that he obtain the money from their stepmother, La Corriveau.

"Dodier responded to their ultimatum by getting drunk. On the morning of April 2, 1763, he began drinking in a Lévis tavern and by midnight was scarcely capable of talking or standing. An old drinking friend, taking pity, loaded him into a cart, drove him out to the mansion in St. Valier, and watched as he staggered into the house. Later, the lone manservant, who was in bed, reported hearing Dodier enter the house and descend to the vast basement kitchen, where he knew La Corriveau would be sitting brooding by the fire, as she often did late into the night. An argument broke out between the couple, louder and more violent than any of the others the servant had overheard. He thought he heard a blow being struck, and this was followed by a shriek from La Corriveau, who afterward came slowly up the stairs to her bedchamber, muttering to herself. As there was no further sound from the kitchen, the servant assumed that Dodier had fallen into his usual drunken sleep on a bench before the fire.

"Sometime later, in the small hours of the morning, the servant was awakened by the sound of La Corriveau leaving her room and going downstairs to the kitchen. He heard logs being thrown on the fire and thought it odd, since he'd never known his mistress to minister to her husband when he came home drunk. He was just drifting back to sleep when a terrible cry — a bellow that quickly turned into a shriek of agony — echoed up through the house. Then there was silence.

"The servant was too terrified to move. Covering his head with the bedclothes, he lay shivering for hours, trying to gain control over his imagination. It was long after dawn before he could summon up enough courage to get out of bed and dress. Slowly, his whole body trembling with fear, he edged his way down the stairs and stepped into the kitchen, which was lit only by the glow of the embers in the wide fireplace. He could barely make out the form of Louis Dodier, who was lying, as he'd often seen him before, on the wide bench before the fire. Then he noticed La Corriveau sitting in her highbacked rocking chair in the shadows beside the hearth, her eyes fixed on the still form of Dodier. She told the manservant that his master had died in the night and instructed him to go to Lévis, where he was to order a coffin from the cabinetmaker and deliver a message she had written to the curé.

"She handed him the message and he immediately ran from the house, saddled a horse, and rode as fast as the animal would go to the house of the curé beside the church in Lévis. The priest was already awake and preparing for an early mass. The servant, still too frightened to speak, wordlessly handed him the message, which simply asked that the curé arrange for the interment of Louis Dodier the following day. Noticing the servant's distress, the curé managed to soothe him by asking a few gentle questions, whereupon the servant managed to gabble out an account of the night's events and his suspicion that Dodier had not died a natural death. The priest immediately sent for one of Dodier's sons, whose farm was less than a mile away. After the son had arrived and heard the servant's story, he insisted that they go to the local English commander, who also served as the civil authority for the township. Three hours later,the English commander, along with a surgeon from his headquarters, and accompanied by the curé, Dodier's son, and the manservant, arrived at the mansion in St. Valier.

"When they descended to the darkened kitchen, they found La Corriveau still seated beside the dead fire, staring at the body of the husband she detested. The commander, who spoke passable French, told her that it was within his authority to order a postmortem examination of the deceased. She remained staring at the body but said nothing. A light was brought and the surgeon bent over the corpse of Louis Dodier. The dead man's face was so contorted that it was obvious he had died in agony, possibly, the doctor thought, from apoplexy or a heart attack, both common enough afflictions in heavy drinkers. But because he had been informed of La Corriveau's reputation, he carefully examined Dodier's mouth for traces or odours of poison. Discovering none, he was about to conclude the examination when he suddenly noticed that the man's left ear, partially concealed by his hair, looked swollen and blistered. With a scalpel he probed the ear and encountered a hard substance. Very carefully, he extracted several metallic fragments that looked like lead. He was puzzled, for he knew it was unlikely that Dodier had been shot. Then his glance happened to rest on the hearth — where, lying amid the ashes, was an iron ladle, and on its inner surface were silvery threads of lead.

"The enormity of his discovery slowly took hold in the surgeon's mind, as he gazed up with horror from the body on the hearth to the wrinkled face of La Corriveau. Lying in a drunken stupor, Dodier had died in agony because molten lead had been poured into his ear. Only one person could possibly have performed that dreadful deed — the woman who sat watching him so silently and malevolently.

"When the English commander charged her with the murder of her husband, La Corriveau made no protest. An escort of soldiers was summoned and took her across the river to the capital, where she was lodged in the Ursuline Convent to await trial. Appalled though the sisters were to have under their roof a reputed witch and the daughter of the notorious Marie Exili, who had been betrothed in that very convent, they treated the accused murderess with respect and charity. In return, although she said nothing, La Corriveau did not try to conceal her utter detestation for her captors. During the week she was confined in the convent, she ate very little, rarely slept, and totally ignored the approaches of an advocate assigned by the authorities to prepare her defense.

"The Governor, General Murray, anxious to impress the local

population with the justice of English rule, himself presided over the tribunal set up to try La Corriveau for murder. Ironically, the trial was held in the large reception room of the convent where, just over a century before, the prisoner's father, Sieur Corriveau, had proposed to her mother. As she was led before the court, La Corriveau, despite her years, still displayed traces of her mother's imperious beauty. Her dark hair, still untouched by gray, tied up in a scarf and dressed in plain black, she carried herself with an erect elegance. There was no sign of deference as she faced the three judges, and when General Murray asked her how she pleaded — guilty or not guilty of the charge presented — she made no reply. Invited to take a seat because of her age, she refused and remained standing.

"The court had summoned more than a dozen witnesses from St. Valier and Lévis, and General Murray and his fellow judges questioned them closely about their testimony. Former friends of Louis Dodier attested to his enmity toward his wife, his sons recalled disputes they had witnessed between the couple, inquisitive neighbours described the violent arguments they had overheard from the mansion in St. Valier, La Corriveau's manservant timidly recounted the events of the night Louis Dodier died, and, finally, the commander from Lévis and his surgeon told of their investigation and discovery of the murder.

"Once again the governor addressed La Corriveau, asking her if she would submit to interrogation, but she merely stared at him with her glittering dark eyes and remained silent. The three judges retired to arrive at a verdict. Within ten minutes they returned and General Murray announced that they had unanimously found Marie Corriveau guilty of the willful murder of Louis Dodier. The governor asked if the prisoner had anything to say before sentence was pronounced. In a low but vehement voice that could be heard in every corner of the large room, La Corriveau spat out, 'I killed Dodier because I hated him, as I hate every one of you here. I hate your kind because you have shown no respect to my mother, to her father, and to those of us who share the powers of the Prince of Darkness. Do what you will to my body now, but be warned — my spirit will live on and will wreak vengeance on you and your kind forever!'

"When the echo of her voice died away, there was an appalled silence in the room for several minutes. Then General Murray rose to his feet and solemnly announced that Marie Josephte Corriveau was to be taken in due course to a place of execution and hanged by the neck until she was dead. La Corriveau listened to his words without emotion and was led from the court to the room where she had been confined.

"The following day workmen began to erect a scaffold at Les Buttes à Neveu, beyond the walls of the city. That evening a curé went to La Corriveau's room and told her that she would be executed at dawn the next day. He pleaded with her to make a full confession of her sins so that he might administer to her the last sacrament. She spat in his face and turned away.

"The dawn was cold, dim, and gray, with rain clouds lowering over the city, when La Corriveau was led from the convent by two English soldiers, her hands bound in front of her, her dark hair uncovered. She was helped into an open wagon, and, although a chair was provided for her, she insisted on standing upright, grasping the rail of the wagon with her bound hands. When the soldiers attempted to support her, she impatiently shrugged off their hands. As the wagon trundled toward the St. Louis Gate, the streets were almost empty. Word of La Corriveau's final warning to the court had passed quickly through the city and most ordinary folk were terrified of exposing themselves to the witch's evil eye. Outside the walls, a safe distance from the grim scaffold on Les Buttes à Neveu, a few carriages were gathered in a cluster, and from within them some society ladies who had once thrilled to La Corriveau's whispered predictions about their loves and their lives watched as their evil confidante approached her death.

"At last the wagon drew up before the scaffold. La Corriveau was lifted down and slowly climbed the steps of the scaffold between the two soldiers. A few officials stood nearby as witnesses to the execution. They lowered their eyes nervously as she, aloof and silent below the gibbet, slowly turned and stared at them. The executioner, who was masked, approached her and asked if she wished him to cover her eyes. She shook her head disdainfully, and he helped her up onto a stool and adjusted the rope around her neck. Had she any last request to make? she was asked. 'Let me be buried,' she said quietly, 'with my own kind on the Ile d'Orléans.' The executioner said nothing, knowing that this would not be possible, and kicked the stool away. For several minutes her body thrashed soundlessly on the end of the rope and then went limp. A military surgeon pronounced La Corriveau dead. The body was cut down and taken back to the convent, along the deserted streets.

"Two days later, according to tradition, the body, chained inside an iron cage, was ferried across the St. Lawrence at night and hung from a tall post at a lonely crossroads near the cemetery between Lévis and St. Valier. The body, still inside the cage, was to hang there for more than fifty years as a grisly warning to those who might be tempted to indulge in witchcraft or murder.

"The considerable fortune that was discovered in La Corriveau's mansion was divided among Louis Dodier's four sons. As none of them, nor any of the local people chose to occupy the deserted house, it crumbled into ruins within a few years.

"That was the end of La Corriveau," said Romeo Dionne, "but really, as I'll tell you, it was just the beginning of the story."

I was startled when he suddenly spoke again in his ordinary, casual voice, and it took me a second or two to realize where I was — back in the present, sitting in a familiar Toronto tavern.

"Good story, eh?" Romeo said with a grin. "Well, you ain't heard nothing yet. I've got to go now and sell off a few more wrecks in the lot. Be here tomorrow, same time, right?"

He gulped down his drink, paid the waitress with the usual flirtatious byplay, and, with a jaunty wave, was gone.

The following evening I was at The Madison before Romeo arrived. He sat down beside me, ordered a drink and lit a cigarette, and without wasting any time took up the story once again.

"Even though St. Valier and Lévis were just across the river from Quebec City, two hundred years ago the folks around there were just simple habitants, devout, superstitious, and with long memories. Thirty years after La Corriveau was executed and hung up in that cage, most of them would avert their eyes if they had to pass the cage at the crossroads during the day, and there weren't many who'd go near the spot after dark. It was just a rusty piece of junk with a few fragments of bone inside, but there were tales of passersby hearing a woman's voice shrieking curses at them.

"Not all the local people were unsophisticated, of course, Dodier's sons, for instance, had all made good use of the fortune they had inherited from La Corriveau. They were well off and they spent quite a bit of money making sure their children received good educations. One of Louis Dodier's grandsons was Joseph Dodier, José for short, whose family home was near Berthier, on the river about five miles downstream from St. Valier. In 1801, he was an eighteen-year-old student at the Jesuit college in Quebec City. Apparently he'd inherited some of his grandfather's liking for good company and strong drink. Whenever school broke up and he was heading home, he would visit the Lévis taverns that his grandfather had frequented many years before. And, of course, he was very familiar with the story of Louis Dodier and La Corriveau, which he'd always considered rather fanciful.

"When school broke up for Christmas that year, he crossed the river in one of the canoes that ferried passengers, halfway on ice and half in open water, between the city and Lévis. True to form, he stopped off at a few of his favourite taverns in Lévis for a little advance festivity. Then, since it was a clear night with a full moon, and since the roads had a good coating of frozen snow on them, he hired a horse and cariole, and set off for home. Although he had had a great deal to drink, he was used to handling a horse, and besides, he was never one to avoid taking a risk. As he approached St. Valier, the notion took him that he should pay his respects to the notorious relative who had contributed so much to his good fortune. As he reached the crossroads, the tall post with its dangling rusted cage stood out clearly in the moonlight. He drew up at the side of the road, dismounted, and walked over to the grisly relic. Opening his fur coat, he took out a flask that he had filled with whiskey back at the last tavern and raised it in a mock toast to the remains of La Corriveau. Then he sat down underneath the cage with his back resting against the post and sipped a little of the fiery spirits as he contemplated the moonlit scene. Below lay the silvery expanse of the river, and beyond that the dark wooded mass of Ile d'Orleans, the Isle of Sorcerers. Surely, he mused, this was a night to bring the evil spirits out for a celebration. Was he just imagining a red glow beyond the trees out there? And what was that? A clink of metal just above his head! Wind? But there was no wind. Suddenly sharp fingers clamped on his shoulder, painful even through his thick coat. He struggled to get up, but could not. The fingers of another hand gripped his other shoulder.

"'Your family owes me a heavy debt, Joseph Dodier,' a rasping voice whispered in his ear. 'Repay it and I will spare you. Take me across to Ile d'Orléans, so that I may be among my own kind. The waters of the river have been consecrated by your accursed priests, and spirits such as I cannot cross unless a Christian like you will carry me. Take me now, or you will die. . . .'

"In agony, José struggled once more to get free. 'No!' he gasped 'No! I won't do it. Let go of me! In the name of . . .'

"Before he could say more, the sharp cold fingers had clawed open his coat and shirt and clenched themselves about his neck. Blackness overwhelmed him.

"When José regained his senses, he found himself lying in the snow below the cage in the dim light of dawn. His flask lay empty beside him. His coat was open and the collar of his shirt was ripped open, exposing the gold crucifix his mother had given him, which was dangling from its chain on his chest. Shuddering with cold and weakness, he slowly struggled to his feet. His neck was painful and stiff and he could feel welts on the skin where hard fingers had bruised it. He did not dare glance at the cage, but he stumbled over to his cariole, climbed in, and whipped up the horse. He did not stop until he had reached the safety of his parents' home at Berthier.

"When José's father saw him draw up before the house and stagger to the door, he assumed that his unruly son had gotten himself into a drunken fight in Lévis. But when the boy babbled out his terrifying story, his father took it very seriously indeed, and so did the local curé, a friend of the family, who was familiar with the legend of La Corriveau. When he had questioned José closely about the incident and examined his bruised neck, he said he was convinced that only the crucifix had saved his life. Fearful that in the future some other unwary traveler might be exposed to the same fate, he proposed immediate action. Late the following night, the priest, accompanied by José's father and elder brother, drove to the crossroads where the cage hung. Flanked by the Dodiers, each of whom held a lighted candle, the priest approached the cage, raised a crucifix, and solemnly began to intone the rite of exorcism. Although it was another windless, clear night, the cage dangling from the tall pole began to shake and clank violently. All three men were terrified, but they managed to control their fear and stood firm. At the point in the ritual at which the priest ordered the unruly spirit to be gone, a harsh, chilling shriek rent the air, continuing for a minute before it died away. The cage, though still swinging on its chain, no longer rattled, and at a signal from the priest, the Dodiers brought tools from their cariole and began digging a deep pit in the frozen earth nearby. Although it was hard work, the fear aroused by the scene they had just witnessed drove them on, but it was dawn before the pit was deep enough. Then they felled the pole and allowed the rusted cage to crash to the ground. With the priest holding his crucifix over it, they cautiously dragged the cage by its chain to the edge of the pit and pushed it in. Then they refilled the pit. The rite of exorcism was repeated over the spot, and then they headed wearily back to Berthier in the cold early light. Before he parted from them at their home, the curé assured them that the accursed spirit of La Corriveau would never again threaten human beings."

Romeo Dionne paused, lit a cigarette, sipped his drink, and contemplated me for a moment. With a shrug, he said, "But of course that priest was wrong, as my grandfather, Roland Dionne, found out seventy years later. But that part of the story'll have to wait till tomorrow. Duty calls. . . . "

As I watched him leave, I couldn't help wondering how much of the story Romeo believed. It occurred to me that if he was as convincing a salesman as he was a storyteller, he must earn a very good living.

Although I made a point of being at the tavern in good time the following evening, Romeo was there before me, obviously eager to continue his story. I'd scarcely had time to order a drink before he began.

"By all accounts, that awful experience at the crossroads sobered José Dodier considerably, and in more ways than one. He persuaded his father to buy him some land near St. Valier, but not too close to the crossroads. He built himself a house and started farming, got married, and had three daughters and a son, Hervé. In spite of the priest's assurance that La Corriveau's spirit was now harmless, José adamantly refused to pass by the spot where the cage was buried. He died, of natural causes, when he was fifty-one, and his son, Hervé, inherited the farm. Hervé married, but as he had no children, he raised his nephew, my granddad, Roland, when his parents were drowned in a storm on the St. Lawrence.

"My granddad must have been a handful when he was young. A bit like José Dodier, I guess, only in his case it wasn't the high life that attracted him — it was wanderlust. In 1868, when he was only fourteen, a big lad for his age, he took off with a traveling theatre company that had been playing in Lévis. Of course his uncle Hervé soon tracked him down and brought him home, but he must have known then that he was never going to keep the lad down on the farm, as the song goes.

"A couple of years later Roland spotted a notice in the local paper about an agent who was visiting Quebec in search of curiosities for the famous Barnum circus. That was just the opportunity my granddad was looking for. He skipped school for a day, crossed the river to Quebec City, and headed for the hotel where the circus agent was staying. As well as looking older than his age, he was very bright and could speak English almost as well as he could speak French. The agent was obviously impressed, because he took the time to listen as this kid told the story of La Corriveau from start to finish, including what had happened to his great-uncle José. The only thing he didn't reveal to the agent was where exactly the cage was buried. He must have had as much chutzpah then as he had when I knew him in his eighties. He offered to produce the cage and La Corriveau's remains if the agent would give him the job of handling it as a sideshow with the Barnum traveling circus. And of course nothing was to get into the newspapers until Roland was actually with the circus. The agent went for the deal, and my granddad arranged all the details for smuggling the cage out of Quebec.

"Three weeks later he met the agent and a couple of roustabouts from the circus in Lévis. He'd borrowed one of his uncle's wagons on the pretext of fetching seed supplies in town, and he'd had a large crate built by a local carpenter. They set off for the crossroads near St. Valier just after midnight, a safe time, since local people were still very nervous about passing the place at night. My gradddad told me afterward that he wasn't too impressed by all the terrible tales his uncle had told him about La Corriveau's powers, but just to be on the safe side he chose a night when the moon was on the wane. He also insisted that each man wear around his neck one of the cheap crucifixes he'd bought in Lévis.

"The crossroad was deserted, as he'd hoped, but even he felt nervous at the prospect of what they intended to do. And it was obvious that the other men would also be glad when the job was finished. Even in the dark he had no trouble finding the place where the cage was buried. His uncle Hervé had shown him the spot, a hummock about ten yards in from the road. They began digging immediately, working very fast, and in less than half an hour one of the shovels struck metal. Five minutes later they uncovered the top side of the cage. It was very badly rusted, and the chain that had once supported the cage broke off when they tugged on it. But with ropes, and using great care, they eased it out of the pit, intact. It would need some restoration and they'd probably have to add to the few fragments of bone that remained inside. They didn't waste any time in sliding it into the crate, loading that onto the wagon, and heading back to Lévis. During the return trip, my granddad remembered thinking that perhaps the curé deserved some thanks for the job he'd done when the cage was buried.

"The sailing boat they had hired was waiting for them at the pier in Lévis and they loaded the crate right away. The wagon and horse were left at a livery stable, along with a note for Roland's uncle that gave no clues as to his nephew's whereabouts. At first light they set sail upstream for Montreal. There they transshipped onto a steamer sailing to Albany, New York, where the Barnum circus was playing at the time.

"According to my granddad, he and P. T. Barnum hit it off right away. Barnum liked people who were pushy, and here was a young guy with a funny accent from the back of beyond who had talked his way into the circus with a bright idea he knew how to exploit. Parts of the old cage were so rotted with rust that they had to be replaced, but a blacksmith was found for the job, as well as a laboratory assistant who supplied a few extra human bones at a reasonable price. It was no problem for my granddad to produce a spiel that would make people's flesh crawl about the horrible career of La Corriveau. More than fifty years later, when I was living with him as a kid, his story could still give me goosebumps. How much he changed and added to the story it's hard to tell, but the way he told it was always convincing. Right from the start, the cage of La Corriveau was a great draw as a sideshow. People love to be scared, and my granddad, Rollie Dionne as they called him, knew how to attract a crowd, roll them up to the ticket booth, and scare the daylights out of them. He had style, and made good money, and that brought him what he liked most — lots of girls wherever he went.

"He traveled with Barnum for more than two years and at the end of it his sideshow was still the talk of the midway. But he was almost too successful. A lot of the other showmen resented this kid, a hick and a greenhorn, drawing off their crowds, and they were jealous of the fact that he was Barnum's favourite. One particular showman, called Brady, who'd been on the carny circuit all his life, really hated my granddad. He was a big, bad-tempered guy who ran the freak show, which is usually the biggest draw, but La Corriveau always outdrew him.

"It all came to a head in 1872, late in the season, when the circus was playing Columbus, Ohio. Brady had had a bad season, and, to make things worse, two of his best freaks had just quit the show. On top of that, he suspected that his wife was fooling around with his rival my granddad. And, between ourselves, she was.

"On their second to last night in town, they'd shut up shop and everyone had gone to bed. Like a lot of the sideshow operators, my granddad had a section partitioned off at the back of his tent, where he slept. That particular night he was finding it hard to sleep, because there was a strong, gusty wind that crackled the canvas of the tents and made the guy ropes creak. He was just drifting off, when he suddenly came awake. He smelled kerosene, followed by smoke. Then he saw a glow of red along the bottom edge of the canvas fly of the partition. He dragged his pants on and ran out into the main tent, where the cage was kept. A Hurricane lamp was lying on its side in the corner and flames from the spilled kerosene were racing up the dry canvas wall. He ran toward the cage to pull it down, but tripped on something. When he looked down he saw a body lying on the ground under the cage. In the light of the flames he barely recognized Brady, who lay with his eyes bulging from their sockets, his tongue protruding from between his lips. As my granddad struggled to lift him, Brady's head lolled back at an odd angle, showing red welts all around the throat. By now the flames were halfway across the roof of the tent, shreds of canvas were showering down on my granddad, and the heat and smoke were unbearable. He knew Brady was dead. So he dropped the body, made a run for it, and fell past the fly, gasping for breath, just as the whole roof caved in. Falling embers had set part of his clothing on fire, so he rolled on the ground to put out the flames, then dragged himself clear of the burning tent. Before he was on his feet again, the wind had driven the fire halfway along the line of sideshows, faster than men could run. There was pandemonium. And before a bucket line could be organized, the big top was gone. In half an hour, most of the animals in the menagerie were lost, a dozen more men were dead, and nothing was left of the circus but a smouldering ruin.

"In the morning they found the remains of Brady's body, crushed and charred where the red-hot cage had fallen on it. As far as anyone knew, Brady was just another victim of the catastrophe. Only my granddad knew that the showman had been the latest victim of La Corriveau. But he didn't tell anyone at the time. Barnum swore he'd build a bigger and better circus, and, as you know, he did go on to do that. But my granddad had had enough. He salvaged the remains of the cage, packed it in a crate, and stashed it in a warehouse. Then he took off on his travels.

"As I told you at the beginning, my granddad roamed the world for most of his life after that. Goldmining, soldiering, whatever. As long as he was on the move, he'd turn his hand to anything. He married three times, tried to settle down each time, but it was never any good. He had my father by his second wife, and, as I said, my dad turned out to be a poor copy of my granddad. I was shuttled around from one relative to another until I finally went to live with my granddad outside Hamilton in 1939. He was sixty-seven then, and if the war hadn't happened I swear he'd have gone on wandering around the world. But somehow he'd gotten himself into the scrap-metal business. We lived in an old farmhouse in the middle of the lot, surrounded by mountains of junk, me, my granddad, and this gorgeous young girlfriend of his, Jenny. It was a great life for a kid. Neither of them minded too much whether I went to school or not, and I had a free run of the lot. Matter of fact, there's where I learned how to fix up cars. I got interested in tinkering with them, and before I was sixteen I'd put together a couple of hot-rods from old cars and sold them off to friends. But the best part of my life was listening to my granddad tell his stories. Because he couldn't roam the world anymore, he loved to talk about where he'd been and what he'd done. You'd only need to sit down with him and he'd be off on a story about the Yukon and Death Valley and Turkey and the Congo. Quite early on I caught on to the fact that he liked to improve on his yarns. Every time he retold a story it'd be different, and usually better.

"Eventually, one day when I was about sixteen, he started telling me about La Corriveau and the cage and his time with Barnum's circus; the story I've been telling you. I could tell that he was very serious about it, but, being a cheeky, spoiled kid by then, I sort of hinted that I thought he was putting me on. That really upset him. And we'd always gotten along pretty good. There was a big old barn behind the house, full of all sorts of junk he thought would come in handy or that he could make a buck on, someday. It was piled up to the rafters. He took me out there and pointed up into the darkness, way high up, and said he still had the cage of La Corriveau and one day he'd prove to me that what he'd told me was true.

"He didn't tell me any more stories after that. But mainly because I'd reached the age when I was more interested in girls than sitting listening to my granddad. I spent most of the time building hot-rods and cruising around Hamilton in them looking for girls. One night in the summer of forty-three I came home late. Jenny was sitting in the kitchen, sobbing her heart out. When she could manage to speak, she told me my granddad was dead. He'd told her he was going out to the barn in the afternoon to sort out some stuff, and when he didn't come in for supper, she went to fetch him. She'd found him lying under a pile of junk that had fallen over on him. He was still alive, and she'd called an ambulance, but he'd died on the way to hospital. Can you guess what was lying on top of him?"

"The cage?" I said.

Romeo nodded. "Yep. La Corriveau's cage."

"So, in the end," I said, "your granddad convinced you that the story about La Corriveau was true?"

He took a sip from his drink and stared into space for a minute or two. "Well, to tell you the truth," he said, "he didn't. To believe in ghosts, you've got to be religious, believe in the hereafter and all that stuff. And frankly, I don't. My granddad, much as I loved him, was a bit of a con artist. Who's to tell how much he invented about La Corriveau? And the fact that that cage fell on him and killed him — couldn't it just be a coincidence?"

He lapsed into silence again. Then he switched back to the familiar persuasive tone that was the tool of his trade.

"But whatever," he said, "isn't that one helluva story? I'd give my right arm to see it in print. You're the writer, so why don't you write it up? Some magazine, maybe one of those American tabloids, would go for a story like that in a big way, right?"

I said they probably would, but with a little too much uncertainty for his taste. He laid a hand on my arm.

"Tell you what," he said quickly. "When my granddad was killed, Jenny and I sold off the scrap yard and split the proceeds. I signed on with the army and went overseas. She took off, probably went back West where she came from, and I lost touch with her. But one thing I held on to was that old cage. I left it with a buddy of mine down in Burlington, and it's still there. Thought at the time that maybe I might get into show business after the war, like my granddad, but I got into the car business instead. Anyway, say I was to bring the cage up here. We could take a few pictures of it and send those in with the story. That'd be a big selling point, eh?"

I felt dubious about the whole idea, but I finally agreed that photographs of the cage would probably help to sell the story. Romeo explained that because things had begun to pile up at work, he wouldn't be able to get down to Burlington until the weekend. He told me he'd call me early the following week so we could make arrangements to photograph the cage, and we shook hands on the deal.

"He didn't call the following week. I continued to drop by The Madison every evening, but he didn't show up there either. Another fast-talker, I thought. Probably there never was a cage and La Corriveau had never actually existed. But just as Romeo himself fascinated me, so did the story, and I wouldn't have felt right about using it without getting his okay. Then it occurred to me to call him. His number was in the directory, but when I called, one of those recorded voices told me that the number was not in service. That pretty well convinced me that I'd been conned. I hadn't actually lost anything, so I just dismissed La Corriveau from my mind and got on with another writing assignment.

A month or so later, I had to go uptown to do an interview. As I came out of the subway I noticed a large used-car lot, the one Romeo had mentioned working in, just across the street. Out of curiosity, I walked over and looked around. There was no sign of Romeo Dionne, but one of the salesmen, younger than Romeo and as flashily dressed, wandered over to me.

"Could give you a really great deal on this one," he said, kicking the tire of the car where I was standing. "One owner and only fifteen thousand miles. Stereo, and a six-month warranty . . ."

"Oh, I'm not in the market," I said. "I was looking for a guy who used to work here. Romeo Dionne."

He looked me up and down for a moment. "You a relative of Romeo's?"

"No, just a friend."

"You haven't heard, then? Got killed in an accident a couple of months back."

"I'm sorry," I said. "What happened?"

"Well, that weekend, he borrowed a pickup off the lot. Said he had something to pick up in Burlington. Next we heard was when the cops called. They said there'd been a smash-up on the 401 Sunday, in the middle of a thunderstorm. Apparently Romeo braked hard, and the load he was carrying slammed into the back of the cab. He ran off the road, flipped over, and the pickup caught fire. He was totalled."

I could only stare at him.

"Really sad," he went on. "Everybody here got along with Romeo. He didn't seem to have any relatives, so the boss paid for the funeral."

"What was he carrying in the pickup?" I asked slowly.

"He owe you something?"

"No, he didn't owe me anything."

"Well, that was the weird thing about it. It was just a load of rusty scrap in a packing case...."

"What happened to it?"

"You're sure he didn't owe you anything?"

I shook my head.

"Well, the pickup and the load were just junk. The towing company wanted to get paid. So the boss told them to sell it for scrap, and paid them the difference. Were you into some deal with Romeo for a car? Because I can give you just as good a deal."

I shook my head again and walked off down the street. Every so often when I watch a car passing by, I think of La Corriveau and that ghastly cage. Is it still lying rusting in some scrap yard, waiting to claim another in its long succession of victims? Or has the rusted iron been swept up into a smelter to take on some other form? Has La Corriveau's vengeance been brought to an end? Or will it go on and on, forever?

11

Fishing

If you want to become a collector, choose something simple. Antique silver spoons, for instance, if you can afford that. Or stamps. Or book matches. Or beer mats. But not ghost stories, which I collect. It's just too frustrating.

The trouble is that you never know when you're getting the genuine article. It's not that it's difficult to come across ghost stories. If you're chatting with friends, at a party say, you've only to mention that you're interested in ghosts and at least one of the people there will say, "Oh, I know a ghost story."

But nine times out of ten, the story will turn out to be one heard from someone else who heard it from someone else again. Hardly ever do you hear a story told by the person who actually encountered a ghost.

And so it seemed with this story, at the beginning. It started with Michael, a veteran police reporter who works for a Toronto radio station. I've known him for a long time, in fact when I was a radio producer he used to work for me. I've always rather enjoyed his cynical tales about low life in the city, about the crooks and cops and lawyers he encounters during his working days, but I never imagined he'd be the source of a ghost story. When he brought it up, I thought he was kidding.

"Got a story for you," he said one day, "a ghost story."

"Sure," I said, "but I've probably heard it fifty times before."

"No," he said without a smile, "the real thing."

"Michael," I said to him, "the only spirits you've ever seen come out of a 26 ounce bottle."

He shook his head. "Didn't happen to me. A cop I know told me the story, or rather an ex-cop. Matter of fact, he works just round the corner from you."

"So tell me," I said, still sceptical.

"No," Michael said, "better you hear it from the guy it happened to. I'll have him give you a call."

The ex-cop's name was Art Dixon. He'd been a detective sergeant with the Ontario Provincial Police. But he'd taken early retirement and found himself a cushy job as security chief with Upper Canada Life, an insurance company that inhabited a dull office tower on Bloor Street East near where I live. Oddly enough, Upper Canada Life is landlord of the aging apartment building where I live and work.

The following morning my phone rang, exactly one minute after nine o'clock, while I was still brooding over my second coffee. "Art Dixon," a clipped voice said. "Michael asked me to give you a call. About a ghost."

I was surprised, because I still suspected Michael of trying to pull some sort to hoax on me.

"I'd be interested to hear your story, Mr. Dixon," I said. "Maybe I could buy you a lunch somewhere close by?"

He hesitated, then said slowly, "Well, it'd be a little awkward in a public place. You see . . . part of the story is on tape. It's the interrogation of a party that was . . . em, implicated with a ghost. It was . . . well, so weird, that I copied it onto a cassette. And I'd want to play that back to you."

That convinced me that I wasn't being kidded.

"Well, Mr. Dixon," I said, I'm just round the corner from you. And I have a cassette recorder. What if you were to come here to my apartment at lunchtime. I could make us some sandwiches. And we could talk in private."

"That'd be fine," he said. "I'll come today, if it suits you. At noon?"

At 12.01 exactly, there was a sharp rap on my front door. Once a cop always a cop, I thought. Dixon was a tall wiry man, with a long weathered face and thinning grey hair, closely cropped. He wore the navy-blue blazer and grey trousers that most security men affect; out of one uniform and into another. He shook hands very firmly and formally.

I'd set a plate of sandwiches, and the cassette recorder, out on the table and I invited him to sit down.

"Can I get you a beer?" I asked him.

He shook his head. "Have to go back on duty," he said.

"A coffee then? I've just made some." He nodded.

While I poured our coffees, we made some small talk about the weather and about my apartment, which has a sort of pokey old charm. Then he said quietly, "This story. It's weird really. Never had anything like it happen to me before. Or since."

I pushed the plate of sandwiches towards him. He took one and chewed reflectively on it for a minute or two.

"I wonder if you'd remember a bullion robbery out at Toronto Airport back in the winter of '76?" he asked me.

"Yes, I do," I said. "I was working in radio news at the time. We covered that. As far as I can recall, the gold was never recovered."

"Matter of fact it was," Dixon said, "a year after the robbery, though we didn't make a big thing of it. And that's part of the story I'm going to tell you."

He stared down at his coffee for a moment.

"Originally that robbery wasn't an OPP matter. The airport is Mountie turf. And the Mounties raised a couple of suspects within 24 hours. The inside man, they thought, was a guy called Clemmie Robichault from Montreal. Had a record as long as your arm, but somehow, under an assumed name, he'd managed to get himself a job in the freight area out at Malton. After the robbery, he just disappeared.

"The outside man I knew myself. Nick Daly, a local and a smart crook. He'd done time, too, break-and-enter, hold-ups, extortion, what have you. Mounties pulled him in a couple of times for questioning. But he had an alibi, sound but phony as hell, and he stuck to it.

"There was no trace of the gold. First off, we thought maybe Clemmie Robichault had holed up with the gold while he negotiated a deal with a fence. We knew that if that much bullion, nearly a million dollars' worth, was smelted and came on the market, we'd hear about it. Because fences, who buy stolen property, are notorious for informing on each other. But there was no word.

"Our only hope was Nick Daly. So we had to keep him under surveillance. He was a slippery customer, and he'd taken to working part-time as a truck driver. So that's how we got involved. The Mounties had to call in the Toronto police and ourselves to keep an eye on him, which was no easy matter.

"The brass upstairs gave us all a hard time, because the insurance people who'd have to pay the tab for what was stolen were on their backs all the time. But by the end of a year, most of us assumed that Robichault had somehow managed to get the gold out of the country and that we'd never see it again."

Dixon took another sandwich and chewed on it.

"One night, it was February 1977," he went on, "a year almost to the day after that bullion heist, I was down at OPP headquarters. Trying to catch up on my paperwork, which is always a real pain. Just to relieve the boredom, I'd walk along to the communications room every so often to see what was coming in on the wire. Around eleven o'clock a report came in from Barrie about some guy in a fishing hut on Lake Simcoe who'd fallen through the ice and drowned himself. His buddy had come in to Jackson's Point on a skidoo to report the accident.

"No big deal, I thought. Never been able to understand guys who'll freeze their asses off to catch a few fish. But then I noticed the names. The guy who'd drowned himself was Nick Daly. And the other guy was a name I knew just as well, Ed Kelly, a small-time crook who was always trying to rip-off milk stores and always got himself caught."

Dixon sighed deeply as though remembering all the petty crooks he'd had to deal with.

"Well, I knew that Daly and Kelly weren't sportsmen," he continued. "Only sport they were ever into was out at Woodbine race-track, losing whatever money they'd managed to steal. Then it struck me. Clever place to stash the bullion — in the lake. Sometimes you get a hunch like that.

"I got onto the duty sergeant at Barrie. He told me they'd sent a man on a skidoo out to the hut on the lake. All he'd found was a big hole in the ice. A lamp, a heater, no fishing gear, and no sign of Daly's body. They were still questioning Ed Kelly, and they'd called out a diving team to see if they could recover Daly's body from the lake.

"I told him what I suspected about the bullion. Then I asked him to book Kelly on suspicion and ship him down town to me in a squad car for interrogation."

Dixon stopped to light a cigarette. I poured him some more coffee.

"They brought Kelly in about one o'clock," Dixon went on. He never was a hero. I knew because I'd collared him a couple of times myself. But he looked real scared that night, face white, sweating like it was July. I put him in an interrogation room and went to get a recorder."

Dixon reached into his pocket and took out an audio cassette. He slipped it into my recorder on the table.

"From the way Kelly was acting, I didn't think I'd have to lean very hard on him to get the real story," Dixon said. Then he pressed down the playback button on the machine.

For a moment or two there were only the sounds of a phone ringing in the background, footsteps and muffled voices. Then there was Dixon's own voice, much more distinct, reciting the usual police caution about anything said being used in evidence. Then Dixon saying more quietly. "Ed, when I saw the report of this so-called accident coming in over the wire, well frankly I was intrigued. Here we have you, Ed Kelly, that's been put away for more penny-ante jobs than I can remember. And we've got Nick Daly, the late Nick Daly so you say, another villain but craftier, who's our prime suspect for a bullion heist at the airport a year ago. And what do we find you two sportsmen doing, Ed? Fishing through the ice. But fishing for what, Ed, fishing for what? Straight away, I had an idea what. You being out there, Ed, was a bit of a puzzle, of course. We know you weren't in on the airport job, because when it was pulled you were doing some time. And we happen to know that Daly's good buddy just then was Clemmie Robichault, who's dropped out of sight, along with that million in gold. And when our guys go out to the fishing hut to investigate this accident you reported, what do they find? A lamp, a heater, no fishing gear. Only a hole in the ice two feet wide. So what were you fishing for, Ed? Sharks? Or maybe it was goldfish, eh?"

A phone rang loudly on the tape, a receiver was picked up and then Dixon spoke again: "Dixon. Oh, Tom. Yes, Mr. Kelly arrived safe and sound. We're just having a little chat here, about fishing. How are things going at your end? They're on their way out, the divers? Great.

Well look, soon as you have anything, give me a call here. Fine. Bye."
The receiver was replaced and then Dixon spoke again: "That was
Barrie, Ed. Couple of divers are on their way out to that fishing hut of
yours. It's my guess they'll find what you guys were fishing for. And
if they can be bothered maybe they'll fish out your pal Nick Daly as
well. We'll probably book you as an accessory, Ed, conspiracy
perhaps, and like as not possession of stolen property. But I warn
you, Ed, if there's a mark on Nick Daly's body, you'll be in real trouble, deep trouble. Maybe first degree."

There was a sort of gasp on the tape, then another voice, a high-
pitched voice, talking very fast, that I guessed was Ed Kelly's: "Jeesus,
sarge, why would I kill him. I never even touched him, I swear to
God. What happened there was weird, real weird. Listen, I'll tell you
what happened, sarge, what really happened...."

Dixon spoke again: "I'm listening, Ed." Then Kelly: "I never
wanted to go out there in the first place . . . Dixon's voice cut in: "Then
why were you out there? Start from the beginning, Ed."

There was a long pause, then Kelly came on again, very tense at
first, the words tumbling jerkily out: "Night before last, Nick called
me. Asked me if I wanted to help him with a problem he had. I knew
Nick. Did some time with him at Kingston. Never did a job with him
though. He wouldn't tell me what he had in mind, only to be on the
corner of Dundas and Parliament seven o'clock the next night, yesterday. So I went along, what the hell. He came cruising along in a car
and picked me up. Never said nothing at first, just headed onto the
Parkway going north. Finally I said to him, where are we going? All
he says is we're going ice-fishing on Lake Simcoe. That really pissed
me off. So I told him I didn't want to go fishing, not in the middle of
winter. So then he just says would twenty-five grand make it more
interesting? I thought about that a while. Then I said maybe it would,
but I'd want to know what I was getting into. Back of my mind was
word I'd heard that Nick had been in on that airport job with the
peasouper you mentioned, Robichault. So I said to Nick, is it the
gold? He just gave a nod. Then he says the law had been on his tail all
year, only tonight he'd managed to give them the slip so's we could go
fishing. I said I didn't see where the fishing came in and all he'd say
was wait and see when we get there."

The tape ran out and as Dixon was changing it, he said, "While we
had the break, I had someone fetch Kelly a coffee, just to calm him
down a bit."

He pushed down the playback button again and his own voice
came on: "So what happened when you got to the lake, Ed?" Kelly
did sound a bit calmer when he answered: "We parked in a boatyard
near Jackson's Point. Nick went into the office and came out again with
a key. There was a skidoo there. He started it up and told me to get on
the back. I only had a short coat on and when we went out on the lake
I thought I was going to freeze to bloody death. We went by a bunch
of fishing huts and then a long way out along the shore to a hut on its

own. When we got there he told me to wait outside a minute till he got the lamp and the heater lit. When he called me in he told me to watch out and not step in the hole. It was a big hole with thin ice on the water. Except for the lamp and the heater, the only other thing was a gaff-hook on a pole. I was shivering so bad that Nick told me to sit down and he gave me a shot of rye he'd brought. So I said to him, well where's this bloody gold? He points and says right down below you, on the bottom. Where Clemmie and me dropped it a year ago. So I said, how do you know this is where it is. The lake's been thawed since. He just laughs and says, because I've got brains. When we dropped it, I got myself a compass and paced the distance out from the shore. Did the same thing a couple of nights ago and marked the place before they towed out the hut. And just to be sure, I rented a metal detector. So how do we get it up, I said, because I didn't see any other gear. He just broke the ice with the gaff-hook, reached in with it under the thick ice and hauled out a float with a rope tied to it. Easy done, he says. Left a lot of wire loops on the package of gold, hooked onto it last night with a grapnell. Too heavy for me to pull up myself, so that's why you're here, he said."

There was a pause on the tape, a long sigh and then Kelly went on: "There was something that was bothering me about the whole set-up, sarge. So I said to him, how come you're bringing me in on this? Why isn't your buddy Robichault here helping you? He gave me a strange look and then he said to me, he is here, Ed, he is here, right under your feet. I asked him what he meant by that. He didn't say anything for a minute, then he handed me the bottle to take another shot. He said, Clemmie and me had a little disagreement the night we brought the gold out to stash it here. Clemmie said he should get a bigger cut when we cashed it in because he'd taken more risks, working out at the airport. I told him no way, a deal is a deal. He pulled a knife on me. I grabbed him. We had a fight. He wasn't a big guy, so in the end I got the knife and... well, it was him or me. Had to get rid of the body though, Ed. So I tied it to the package of gold and dropped 'em both into the water. ..."

Dixon's voice came on the tape again, saying quietly, "So that's how Clemmie Robichault dropped out of sight. No wonder we couldn't trace him. Here, Ed, better have a cigarette." There was the click of a lighter, then Dixon again: "Heavy stuff, Ed. So what did you do then?" Kelly, sounding very tense, answered: "I told him I didn't want any part of the deal. Not with murder. Not with pulling that body out with the gold. He told me there was no way I could back out now. But anyway, he said, he'd double the offer, fifty grand. Just to make his point, he opened his coat and showed me he was carrying a gun. And he said that there wouldn't be any body left, the fish would have eaten it. Didn't see that I had much choice, sarge. Had to do what he said. He hooked a loose end of the rope out of the water and we both began pulling up the gold. It was real hard going, specially since we didn't have much room in the hut. He was nearest the hole and I was behind him. ..."

On the tape, Kelly was beginning to sound very shaky, almost as though he was pulling on that rope again, breathing heavily: "Every now and then we'd have to stop for a breather and Nick'd lean over and look into the water. Didn't think we'd ever make it, sarge. Then he said, we're nearly there, Ed, I can see it. Couldn't see much myself, because I was behind him. Then he said hold on tight and he knelt down. I saw something in there, and then, I swear to God, sarge, these two white things, hands, came out of the water and grabbed Nick round the neck. There was a big splash and he was gone. I had to let go of the rope or the weight would have pulled me in too. I swear to God, sarge, that's exactly what happened, I swear. . . ."

The only sound on the tape was Kelly sobbing. A phone rang and a receiver was picked up. Then the sergeant's voice: "Dixon. You have? Quick work." A long pause, broken only by Dixon saying, "Yes . . . yes. . . ." Finally Dixon saying, "Well, that's great. Let me know what the coroner's people have to say. Yes, I'll be here."

The receiver was put down and there was a long silence, with an occasional sob from Kelly. Then Dixon said slowly, "Ed, before that telephone rang I was going to give you a bawling out for trying to con me with a story like you just told me. That was the sergeant in charge of the diving team. They'd just come in off the lake. And do you know what they found out there? Just like you said, they found the package of bullion. They found Nick Daly's body, with a gun stuck in his belt. And they found the remains of a body on the bottom, only bones, that might have been Clemmie Robichault's. And I'll tell you what else they found, Ed. We can't be sure of this till the coroner examines Nick's body, but it looks very much like he wasn't drowned. Looks as though he was throttled by someone, or something, marks round the throat, tongue out, all the signs. . . .

Kelly's voice babbled suddenly on the tape: "I told you, sarge, I told you that's what happened. I swear to God . . ." Dixon's voice cut him short: "Calm down, Ed, calm down. We got a problem here that we've got to work out.

There was another silence on the tape. I noticed that Dixon was looking slightly uneasy as he waited. His voice on the tape was very deliberate when it resumed: "Ed, there's no way we're going to go into court and be made to look like a bunch of assholes. What's the prosecutor going to tell the judge, that Nick Daly was killed by someone that's been dead for a year? Even if we were to charge you with possession of stolen goods, there'd be questions, awkward questions. . . ."

Kelly interrupted: "I never even seen that gold, sarge." Dixon cut him short again: "Cool it, Ed, hear me out. We could take a chance and try charging you with the murder. But look at you, Ed. Nick Daly was nearly twice your size, and a known tough guy, carrying a gun. So is any jury going to believe that you jumped him, throttled him and dumped him into the lake? No way."

After another long pause, Dixon went on: "Tell you what, Ed, I've cautioned you already and by rights I should advise you to get yourself a lawyer. But between ourselves, the less people we have in on this the better for everybody. When we get the coroner's report, to my mind, we can probably make a deal, a deal that'll leave you home free."

Dixon leaned over and switched off the machine, then he lit a cigarette. Plainly embarrassed, he shrugged and said to me, "You're a writer and you probably think that's a great story. I'm a cop . . . was a cop and so my job at the time was to uphold respect for the law."

"And so what happened?" I asked.

"What I suspected was confirmed by the autopsy," he said. "Nick Daly had died of strangulation. The thorax ruptured, a line of contusions round the flesh of the throat. . . ." He stretched out his two hands, ". . . as might have been caused by fingers. Fingers without any flesh on them. . . , ."

He stared at his own hands for a moment or two, then pulled himself together and said in a matter-of-fact voice, "With very little publicity, we contrived a verdict of death by misadventure in Daly's case. Dental records and a stab wound in the skull confirmed that the bones belonged to Clemmie Robichault. Again, death by misadventure."

"And the bullion?" I asked. He gave me a wry smile.

"Quietly returned to the airline that had lost it. They didn't want the public reminded they'd been robbed by a couple of smalltime crooks. And the insurance people were happy to go along with that."

He reached over and removed the cassette from the machine, and added ruefully, "As for ourselves, it could have been a triumph of law enforcement. But we could never admit that we owed it all . . . to a ghost."

He tapped the cassette against his fingernails.

"Naturally," he said, "we wiped the original tape. And I'll probably wipe this, too. Just wanted someone else to hear it. But, of course, I'd have to deny ever having met you, if I was asked."

"Don't worry," I said. "Names and details can be altered. Nobody expects ghost stories to be proven beyond doubt."

He slipped the cassette into his blazer pocket and stood up, adding, "Even now, I'm still not sure I believe in ghosts."

As I walked him to the front door of my apartment, I said, "But Ed Kelly, what happened to him?"

"He wasn't charged, of course," said Dixon. "But the experience seems to have straightened him out, almost. Works as a salesman for one of those companies, just inside the law, that hustles cheap gold-plated jewellry as the real thing."

As we shook hands at the door, he added, "One thing I can tell you for sure. Eddie doesn't go fishing in his spare time. You won't believe this. He dabbles in spiritualism."